MURDER, SHE WROTE:
MANHATTANS AND MURDER

MURDER, SHE WROTE

Manhattans & Murder

Jessica Fletcher and Donald Bain

Chivers Press • G.K. Hall & Co.
Bath, England • Thorndike, Maine USA

This Large Print edition is published by Chivers Press, England, and by G.K. Hall & Co., USA.

Published in 1998 in the U.K. by arrangement with Universal.

Published in 1998 in the U.S. by arrangement with Chivers Press, Ltd.

U.K. Hardcover   ISBN 0–7540–3285–X (Chivers Large Print)
U.K. Softcover   ISBN 0–7540–3286–8 (Camden Large Print)
U.S. Softcover   ISBN 0–7838–0133–5 (Nightingale Series Edition)

A novel by Jessica Fletcher and Donald Bain based on the Universal television series created by Peter S. Fischer, Richard Levinson & William Link

The text of this Large Print edition is unabridged.
Other aspects of the book may vary from the original edition.

Set in 16 pt. New Times Roman.

Printed in Great Britain on acid-free paper.

British Library Cataloguing in Publication Data available

Library of Congress Cataloging-in-Publication Data

Bain, Donald, 1935-
    Manhattans & murder / Jessica Fletcher & Donald Bain.
    p. (large print) cm.
    ISBN 0-7838-0133-5 (lg. print : sc : alk. paper)
    1. Large type books.   I. Title.
[PS3552.A376M36   1994]
813'.54—dc21   98-14731

CHAPTER ONE

It was his eyes.

Not that his eyes caused me to stop and look at him. The red Santa Claus suit, shiny black boots and fake, grizzled white beard did that. But it was his eyes that sparked recognition in me.

He was one of a dozen solicitors of charitable contributions on Fifth Avenue that crisp, sunny day in December. Some employed loud musical accompaniment as they attempted to woo hordes of pedestrians passing each hour, a few hopefully imbued with the Christmas spirit of giving. The Santa Claus I stopped to observe had only a small, cheap bell, whose tintinnabulation could barely be heard over the blaring, out-of-tune brass ensemble of an adjacent Salvation Army unit.

He didn't seem to notice me as I stood in front of Saks Fifth Avenue's festive holiday windows. Why would he? I was only one of countless faces on the street at that hour. Besides, it had been at least ten years since Waldo Morse and I had last seen each other. It probably wasn't even Waldo.

Still, I couldn't resist having a closer look. I pulled a dollar bill from my purse, navigated the stream of foot traffic at the risk of being

1

bowled over, and dropped the money into a cardboard box decorated with shimmering red and green paper that sat at his feet.

'Thank you,' he mumbled, his eyes looking beyond me.

'Merry Christmas,' I said loud and clear. I didn't move, and my presence compelled him to acknowledge me. He stopped ringing the bell and frowned. 'Waldo?' I said.

The mention of his name seemed to rattle him. He glanced away, rang his bell one more time, then looked at me again. 'Jessica Fletcher.' He said it in a hoarse whisper as though trying to keep others from hearing.

'Yes, it's me, Waldo. What an incredible surprise. No, shock is more like it.'

It suddenly occurred to me—too late, as is usually the case—that I'd been imprudent in openly approaching him. His expression confirmed it. He was overtly uncomfortable, and I wished I could reverse my actions of the past few minutes, run the movie backward.

I was now as awkward as he was uncomfortable. I said cheerily, 'Well, Waldo, they say you always bump into someone you know in this big city. I guess they're right. Nice to have seen you.' I was about to rejoin the stream of pedestrians moving uptown when he said, 'Mrs Fletcher. Wait.'

I turned. Was he smiling beneath the white beard? Hard to tell, but I felt better thinking he was. I moved closer as he said in that same

2

whisper, 'I'd like to talk to you.'

He looked left and right; he seemed anxious to keep our conversation private. No need to worry about that, not with the Salvation Army brass orchestra groaning loudly through *Adeste Fideles*.

'Come back tomorrow,' he said. 'Meet me here at two.'

'Two? Oh my, I'm afraid I—' I stopped myself. The plans I'd made for the next afternoon could be juggled, even shelved. I would not, could not, pass up the chance to talk to Waldo Morse. 'I'll be here at two sharp,' I said.

I walked to the corner of Fiftieth Street, stopped, and looked back over my shoulder. As I did, a priest who'd come from the direction of St. Patrick's Cathedral approached Waldo. The transaction didn't go the way I assumed it would. Instead of the priest's putting money into the box at Waldo's feet, Santa Claus handed the priest something.

The priest quickly disappeared into the crowd. Waldo snapped his head in my direction and saw that I'd observed what had taken place. I rounded the corner and headed east. Somehow, I felt I should not have witnessed the exchange between them. Why? I wasn't sure. Maybe because of who Waldo Morse was, and the reason he'd departed Cabot Cove.

Tomorrow at two. I'd be there.

3

CHAPTER TWO

'Well, Jessica, how was your first full day in Gotham?'

'I'd forgotten how exhausting walking around Manhattan can be,' I replied to my publisher of many years, Vaughan Buckley, in whose spacious apartment I sat, stockinged feet propped up on a blessed ottoman, a glass of sparkling mineral water with lime in my hand. Vaughan's wife, Olga, was in the kitchen making canapés. Their dogs, Sadie and Rose, were curled up together on a cushioned window seat.

'Accomplish all your shopping?' Buckley asked as he pulled a tufted red leather chair to the other side of a glass coffee table.

I laughed. 'Heavens, no. I haven't even begun my own shopping. When friends in Cabot Cove knew I'd be in New York this Christmas, they all wanted me to bring something special back to them. I told them I was staying through New Year's Eve, but that didn't deter them. They said a gift bought in a fancy New York shop would make up for giving it late.'

'And, there's also the panache of having the world's most famous mystery writer personally buy it for them.'

'No, I don't think so,' I said, sipping my drink. 'I just hope my feet hold up.'

Olga Buckley came from the kitchen carrying our snacks on a blue-and-white Daum serving plate. Antiques and gourmet cooking were her passions; she was well versed in both subjects. Their apartment, all twelve rooms of it, was as handsomely turned out as its owners. Vaughan and Olga Buckley were attractive people, Nautilus-thin, beautifully groomed, and impeccably dressed on all occasions. She'd been a successful model when she'd met the young editor who would go on to found one of publishing's most respected houses.

The apartment was on the ninth floor of the Dakota on West Seventy-second Street, famous for all the artistic community's leading lights who'd called it home since it was built in 1884. It had been the setting for the horror movie *Rosemary's Baby*, and rendered infamous when former Beatle John Lennon was murdered in its courtyard by a deranged fan in December of 1980.

I'd been to the apartment before as a dinner guest, but had never stayed there, although I had a standing invitation whenever I visited New York. This time, they'd been especially persuasive. Olga said she would not hear of me staying in a hotel, and Vaughan even threatened (in jest, I assume and hope) to shortchange me on royalties the next time they came due. I was glad they'd prevailed.

5

Although our relationship was the result of my writing books for Buckley House, they'd become what I considered good, dependable friends.

Olga sat next to her husband. 'So, Jessica, tell us what you did today,' she said.

My first thought was of having bumped into Waldo Morse. I wanted to share that with them, along with the strange circumstances of Waldo's life, but thought better of it. Maybe after meeting with him the next day, but not now. Practicing discretion seemed the best thing I could do for Waldo at this point.

Instead, I told them of shops I'd visited in search of items on my Cabot Cove shopping list. I'd barely made a dent. 'Our sheriff, Morton Metzger, collects toy soldiers,' I said. 'I think I've mentioned him to you before. He asked me to go to a shop with a funny name and buy him a certain soldier that's missing from one of his regiments.' I picked up my purse from the floor in search of the card I'd been given at the shop, but Olga quickly said 'Funchies, Bunkers, Gaks and Gleeks.'

'You know it.'

'Yes. The owner and I are friends. I love the shop. Did you find the soldier?'

'I certainly did. One item checked off my list.'

'Always a good feeling,' Buckley said. 'Want to nap before dinner, Jess? Our reservation is at seven, and doing the Larry King show will

6

turn this into a very long day for you.'

I stretched and let out a contented sigh. 'A nap sounds lovely. Sure you don't mind?'

'Not at all,' said Olga. 'I think I'll take one myself.'

I knew I wouldn't sleep, but an hour of solitude and quiet was appealing. My room was large and faced the central courtyard. Through my window I could see the balconies of other apartments, all the lovely oriel windows, turrets, gables, finials and flagpoles. The Dakota was a mix of architectural styles, some German, a little French, certainly English Victorian. It was now dark; patches of yellow light from other windows were warm and inviting.

My room looked much as it probably had when the building went up. It was furnished with a handsome selection of antiques to go with the carved marble mantel above my fireplace, walls of mahogany paneling and marble floor. A large, rich red-and-gold Oriental rug covered the center of the room. My king-size bed was canopied. I love the look but can never stop wondering how much dust has accumulated on top.

I slipped out of my clothes, put on a robe, and sat at an antique French desk near the window. I tried to focus upon all the wonderful aspects of this trip to Manhattan, but found it difficult. I'd always wanted to spend a Christmas in bustling New York City—

although Cabot Cove, as small as it was, generated its own sense of holiday urgency and pace. I usually celebrated Christmas and the passage into a new year at home. But this year the early November publication of my latest murder mystery triggered an intense publicity effort by Buckley House. Vaughan Buckley saw the book as a perfect Christmas gift and prevailed upon me to head south for media appearances, newspaper interviews, and autographing sessions at bookstores. I was absolutely shocked, of course, when they told me I would be a guest on the Larry King Show. I'd always been a fan of Mr King, but never thought he would be interested in having a mystery writer as a guest. I was wrong. Tonight, I would meet the talented TV host and do my best to sound intelligent.

I'd originally intended to return to Cabot Cove the day after Christmas, but the persuasive Mr Buckley, along with other friends in Manhattan, had convinced me to celebrate New Year's Eve with them. This didn't set well with my friends in Maine.

'New Year's Eve won't be the same without'cha,' Seth Hazlitt, my physician friend, said when I announced my plans. 'Trudy promised to make a batch of her Chicken Roly-Poly, Ms Haines's been promisin' a big round 'a molasses taffy, and the club says it saved enough over the year to bring up a real band from Portland. We never had real live music before.'

It wasn't easy for me to break tradition and to disappoint Seth, but I was committed. My concession was a promise to call the Cabot Cove Citizen Center at midnight to wish my friends a happy new year.

I looked at the list of presents I was asked to buy while in New York but couldn't concentrate on that, either. The chance meeting with Waldo Morse dominated my thoughts. In a way, I was sorry I'd seen him. Better to let unpleasant episodes from the past stay just that—in the past. On the other hand, my natural curiosity, which friends have occasionally characterized as putting cats to shame, made me want the hours between now and two o'clock the next day to pass quickly. What would he tell me? What had his life been like all these years?

Oh, well, I thought, as I headed for the large marble bathroom. One thing at a time, Jess. Shower, dinner, the TV show, a good night's sleep, sign books at B. Dalton in the morning, lunch with a reporter from *Newsday*, and then back to Fifth Avenue.

My curiosity about Waldo Morse would be sated soon enough.

CHAPTER THREE

'Say something in Maine,' instructed one of the last callers to me on the Larry King Show.

'Pardon?'

'You know, talk funny like people in Maine do.'

'People in Maine don't talk funny,' I said. 'People in New York talk funny.'

Larry King giggled. 'Come on,' he said. 'You know what the caller means, Jessica. Put the cah in the garage.'

I laughed. 'What a strange thing that would be, putting a car—or a *cah* as you pronounce it—in a garage. In Maine, a car is a big underwater crate where lobsters are stored live until they're shipped.'

'Really?'

'Yes.' I didn't want to be combative, or a spoilsport, and so I was about to politely continue the conversation when the caller suddenly identified himself as Cabot Cove sheriff Morton Metzger. 'Jess,' he said, 'I figured if Bill Clinton's mother could call in when Clinton was a guest, I could, too.'

'But you're not my mother,' I replied. King laughed. Morton wanted to continue talking but the smooth, adept talk show host nicely and quickly put an end to Morton's fifteen minutes of fame. I was pleased to know that my friends in Cabot Cove were watching, and was glad Morton had called.

When the show was over, Vaughan, Olga, and the publisher's publicity director, Ruth Lazzara, assured me I'd been 'a smash.' I wasn't so sure they were right. It had gone by so quickly, I had trouble remembering anything that happened on the set.

I got to bed at midnight and slept fitfully. I didn't know whether it was the remnants of the heavy dinner we'd had, the tension of being a guest on a national television show, or lingering thoughts about my scheduled rendezvous the next day with Waldo Morse. No matter what the cause, a sound sleep evaded me that night.

I was up earlier than my host and hostess, quietly made a cup of coffee, and read the *New York Times* they told me would be at the door.

They joined me an hour later. Eventually Ruth Lazzara, a vivacious young redhead with a seemingly bottomless reservoir of energy, picked me up at the appointed time and took me to B. Dalton, where I was amazed to see a hundred people lined up in anticipation of my appearance, many of whom said they'd seen me on the Larry King Show. There were tall stacks of my book on a table, and I was to autograph one for each person in line who purchased a copy. Ruth whispered to me before we started. 'While you have a minute, Jessica, try and sign them all. The store can't send back signed books.'

'I couldn't do that,' I said. I knew what she was getting at. Books are sold to stores on a consignment basis, one of the few industries left that operates that way. A store can send back for full credit any book it doesn't sell unless, of course, it's been signed.

The publicity director laughed. 'It's done all the time, Jessica.'

'Yes, I'm sure it is, but not by me.'

'Whatever you say.' Her tone was less bubbly than before.

It all turned out nicely. They sold sixty books, and the people I met were friendly. I had one whimsical moment when I considered asking them to 'say something New York,' but I resisted the temptation.

Ruth escorted me to my lunch with the *Newsday* reporter, another lively young woman who obviously hadn't read my book—any of my books—but who wasn't deterred by that. I hadn't had breakfast and was ready for lunch, especially good Italian food (somehow, Hick's Leaning Tower of Pizza in Cabot Cove never satisfied my love of pasta and spicy veal dishes). We lunched at Antolotti's, a lovely Italian restaurant on Forty-ninth Street and First Avenue where my picture was taken with the owner to join other celebrity photos on the walls.

After salads had been served, I was bombarded with questions from the reporter about my work habits. By the time we got around to coffee, she told me she was working on a murder mystery and wondered if I would take a look at it, perhaps even collaborate with her.

'It's kind of you to ask,' I said, 'but I don't collaborate.'

'Maybe you could read it and give me some advice.'

I managed to sidestep that awkward situation by encouraging her to keep writing, giving her some general tips on submitting manuscripts for publication, and slipping her final questions about my personal life, my deceased husband, and whether I had any current romantic interests. I naturally thought about George Sutherland, the handsome and charming Scotland Yard Inspector I'd met in London the year before, but didn't mention him. You couldn't call our relationship 'romantic,' although I did think of him often, and had received some letters over the past year. A nice man. A gentleman. 'Say something funny in Scottish,' I thought, smiling to myself. 'No,' I said to the interviewer as we stood outside the restaurant, 'there are no romantic interests in my life at this time.'

The minute she turned the corner, I jumped in a cab. 'Fifth Avenue and Fiftieth Street, please,' I told the driver, whose only acknowledgment was to slap on the meter and jam his foot down on the accelerator pedal.

Why he bothered to accelerate fast was beyond me. It was slow-going, the holiday season in Manhattan having brought thousands of extra cars into the city.

Hopelessly mired in traffic at Forty-ninth and Madison, I paid the driver and walked the rest of the way to my rendezvous with Waldo. Frankly, I didn't think he would be there, but I was wrong. There he was, ringing his little bell and tossing in an occasional 'Ho, ho, ho.'

I stood in front of the same Saks window and watched the parade on Fifth. There seemed to be even more people, if that were possible. A few passersby fought the flow and managed to drop change into the box at Waldo's feet. I was certain Waldo hadn't seen me arrive. At least he did nothing to indicate he had.

I instinctively reached into my purse and pulled out a small point-and-shoot camera that I always carried with me. For a moment—and it lasted no more than that—I questioned the propriety of taking a picture of Waldo. But it wasn't a decision I had to make. I simply raised the camera to my eye, waited for a break in the foot traffic, and took the photo. He still didn't seem to notice me. I heard the film automatically advance in the tiny technological marvel in my hands and was about to take another frame when it happened. It was instantaneous; a flash point of time. Sound. Motion. Horror.

I couldn't see the face of the person who

stepped up to Waldo, pressed a revolver into his stomach, and squeezed the trigger, nor did I think to keep my eye on him or her. The mind doesn't always process information quickly enough to instantly do the right thing. At least mine doesn't.

Now, a scream from a woman who saw Waldo slump to the ground. The camera was still to my eye, and I took another picture. At this point, Waldo was lying on his side on the pavement, his fake beard pushed up and covering most of his face. Blood dripping from his mouth quickly turned the beard to pink. Other people stopped. I'd forgotten about the person who'd shot Waldo. Where had he gone? Was it a he? I'd only seen the back of a figure from a three-quarter angle. The person wore a stocking cap and scarf brought high up around his, or her, chin, masking features. The coat was black. A raincoat. And the killer was gone. Disappeared.

Waldo wasn't dead yet. His right hand clutched for something unseen. Life, perhaps. Now my mind caught up with the action. Someone had shot Waldo Morse, right there on Fifth Avenue, in New York City, at two o'clock in the afternoon at the height of the Christmas season.

'Oh, my God!' I said, attempting to push through the crowd that had stopped to gawk at the fallen Kris Kringle. I fell to my knees and reached through legs that separated me from

15

him. 'Waldo, Waldo,' I said, my fingertips touching his beard. I couldn't see him, but one of his hands gripped mine. I looked up into the faces of the men and women witnessing his death. 'Please, do something,' I said. 'Get help. Call the police. Call an ambulance.' But I knew it was too late. As I implored those surrounding me to act, his grasp loosened and his hand fell to the cold Manhattan pavement.

I slowly stood and extended my hands in a gesture of utter helplessness and frustration. Then, I saw him, not the person who'd shot Waldo, but the priest I'd seen the previous day. He was short and stocky, and his complexion was swarthy.

I started to say something to him, but as I did, his face turned sour. He had black eyes that bore into me. He turned and walked away.

'Father,' I shouted, 'Father . . .' My words had no effect. He was gone, swallowed by the throng of humanity that was Fifth Avenue that December day.

CHAPTER FOUR

A police car arrived, and three men got out. Two wore uniforms; the other was a plainclothes detective. Fast, I thought. They must have been passing by. They moved the large crowd back, and one of them crouched

16

and pressed fingertips against Waldo's neck. He looked up at the detective and shook his head.

'Anybody see what happened here?' the detective asked in a loud, surprisingly high voice. He was short and compact; dark, thin hair trailed upward in wispy curls.

There were no responses. Most people who'd witnessed the murder had walked away.

'Nobody saw nothing?' he asked, louder this time.

'I did,' I said. The words came from me as though spoken by someone else. The detective turned in my direction and frowned. 'You saw him get shot?'

'Yes, I did.' I approached. 'So did a lot of other people,' I said.

The detective looked into other faces. Some of the people belonging to them shrugged and shook their heads. 'I didn't see anything,' a man said. 'Nothing,' said a woman. 'I just got here.'

'This is outrageous,' I said, looking directly at those I knew had witnessed the murder. 'Don't any of you have a sense of civic responsibility?' I'd heard stories of New Yorkers' penchant for looking the other way, but this was ridiculous.

They looked at me as though I were demented. Most left. Heavy with guilt, I hoped. I said to the detective, 'My name is Jessica Fletcher. I was here when this man was shot.'

'You saw it happen? You saw everything?'

'Well, not everything, but enough. I saw who shot him.'

'You did?'

'Not to the extent that I could identify the person, but I did catch a glance. It was ... I think, it was a man, although, I admit, it could have been a woman.'

The detective's pained expression mirrored his thoughts. Of course, his expression might have passed for sweetness if he knew that not only did I know the victim, I'd come to this street corner specifically to meet with him.

I'd gone through an internal debate about telling the police what I knew about Waldo Morse but decided to wait. Not there, not with his body on a slab of cement in front of Saks. It wasn't only a question of place and time, however. Waldo's life since leaving Cabot Cove had been anything but routine. Because it involved elements of secrecy—and danger—I hadn't wanted to place him in physical jeopardy. That's why I'd been so circumspect in approaching him initially. But as I looked down at his lifeless body, I knew such concern was all academic now. Yes, I'd tell the police what I knew. But later. Time and place.

I'd also made a snap decision about the photographs I'd taken. I would have the film developed. If the pictures showed anything that might be of help to authorities, I would turn them over. Not before.

As the detective jotted in a small notebook,

an Emergency Medical Services ambulance parted the heavy traffic with its piercing siren and joined the patrol car at the curb. A young man and woman in white uniforms jumped from the vehicle. The detective raised his hand. 'Take it easy,' he said. 'He's a stiff.'

His words assailed me. I didn't like the way he'd referred to the body. Waldo deserved more dignity than that. I didn't say anything, however. I didn't need a detective berating me.

I watched with a mixture of horror and relief as the medical personnel wrapped Waldo's body in a soiled sheet, placed it on a stretcher, and slid it into the back of the ambulance.

'All right, all right, everybody move on. The show is over,' the detective said. Then, to my amazement, they climbed back into their patrol car.

I ran up to it. 'Officer! Don't you want to question me as a witness?'

He looked at me with that same sour expression. 'Lady, it's not like the mayor got killed here.'

'I don't believe this,' I said. 'A man has been murdered. I was a witness. You can't just drive away.'

One of the officers in the front seat laughed. I said in a louder voice, 'I insist upon giving a statement.' I wasn't sure I should be insisting upon anything, but didn't know what else to do. The police do not just walk away from a witness to a murder.

Do they?

The driver had started the engine. The detective told him to shut it off, opened the door, and invited me to join him in the back. I looked around. Dozens of people, most of them newcomers to what had happened, watched. I managed a weak smile and joined him in the car.

'Name?' the detective said, a notebook in his left hand, a pen in his right.

'Jessica Fletcher.'

'What accent is that?'

'Accent? I'm from Maine. Cabot Cove, Maine.'

'What are you doing in New York?'

'The same thing many people are doing, visiting friends and doing Christmas shopping.' He wrote the words 'Maine' and 'Christmas shopping' on his pad.

'What did you see?' he asked.

'I saw . . . I was standing on the corner when a man . . . or, as I said, possibly a woman . . . stepped up to the Santa Claus, put a gun in his stomach, and pulled the trigger.'

'Description of alleged assailant?'

'Medium height, wore a stocking cap and a scarf brought up high around the chin.' I demonstrated with my hands. 'He, or she, wore a black raincoat.'

'You see the color of the hair? Eyes? Skin?'

I ruefully shook my head.

'Where did the alleged assailant go after

he—or she—pulled the trigger?'

'I don't know. It happened so fast. The person was there, and then he or she wasn't.'

'No idea?'

'No. No idea.'

The detective closed the notebook and put it in his pocket. 'Well, thank you, Mrs Fletcher, for coming forward. You've been very helpful.' His sarcasm was not lost on me.

'Don't you want to know how to reach me?' I asked.

'Maine. What town did you say it was?'

'Cabot Cove, but I'm staying in New York through the new year.'

'Well, have a nice day. Welcome to the Big Apple.'

'May I have your name and badge number, please?' I took out my own notebook and pen.

He stared at me.

'I'd like to be able to contact you to see how things are progressing with this case. After all, I did witness the murder. I think I'm entitled to that courtesy.'

His sigh was deep. 'Rizzi,' he said. 'Alphonse Rizzi. Badge number one-three-nine-zero, Detective. Narcotics.'

I wrote it down and thanked him. 'I'm sure you won't mind my calling to check on your progress.'

'I'll really look forward to it, Mrs Fletcher.'

I was expected to leave the car, and did. I stood at the curb and watched it pull away, my mind still bewildered by what I considered to be an appalling lack of professional interest on the part of the police. It was beyond me that they could take so cavalier a position where not only had a murder taken place in their city, the victim had been a sidewalk Santa Claus collecting money for the needy. I've always understood the need for police to assume a detached, perhaps even callous attitude toward death—like doctors and nurses—but this man had carried it to extremes.

As I watched the patrol car wind its way through the heavy traffic, someone tapped my shoulder. I turned and looked into the eyes of a young man wearing a red-and-black plaid jacket and yellow earmuffs. He hadn't shaved in days; he had the Don Johnson look, which I thought had gone out with the Eighties.

'You photographed the murder,' he said.

'Pardon?'

'Somebody told me you took pictures while it was happening.'

'Whether I did or not is none of your business.'

He smiled. 'Maybe it should be. Look, I'm with the *Post*. This could be a big story, especially if we've got a dynamite photo for Page One.'

'Well, that may be true, but you won't get any "dynamite photo" from me.'

I started to move past him, but he blocked my way. 'Don't I know you from some place?'

he asked.

'I'm sure you don't,' I said, attempting once again to leave but finding my progress impeded.

'Yeah, I know who you are. Jessica Fletcher. I saw you on the Larry King Show last night.'

'That has nothing to do with whether I took pictures or not.'

'Are you kidding, Mrs Fletcher? If the famous Jessica Fletcher, big-time murder mystery writer, actually took pictures of a Santa Claus getting iced on Fifth Avenue in front of Saks, that is a very big story.' He strung out the final words.

'What is your name?' I asked.

'Johnson. Bobby Johnson.'

'Well, Mr Johnson, I admire your tenacity as a journalist, but I'm afraid we have nothing to talk about.'

I walked as quickly as I could, which wasn't easy with the holiday crowds, and stopped occasionally to glance over my shoulder. Sure enough, Mr Johnson was following. After I'd gone a few blocks, I paused at a corner, waited for him to catch up and said as sternly as possible, 'Mr Johnson, I did not take any photographs. But if I did, I would not share them with you to create a lurid front page for your newspaper. Understood?'

'Give me a break, Mrs Fletcher. I've been dry for too long. I need a piece like this. The paper pays good for pictures. If we could get an exclusive, first-hand account from you of the murder, they'll really put up bucks. Besides, you're here promoting your new book. You could do worse than the front page of the *Post*.'

'You're right,' I said pleasantly, 'but I'd rather never sell another book than use the murder of a . . .' I'd almost said old friend and was relieved I hadn't. 'Good-bye, Mr Johnson.'

A taxi pulled up and a couple got out. I quickly got in, slammed the door, and told the driver to take me to the Dakota. Johnson stood on the curb, a big smile on his face, which said many things, including that he would find out where I was staying while in New York, which is not difficult for a good journalist with connections. I dwelled on that probability for a block or two until thoughts of Waldo Morse took over, and the grimy backseat of a New York taxi, driven by a madman with a lead foot, was filled with memories.

CHAPTER FIVE

By the time I reached the apartment and had received my customary warm wet welcome from Sadie and Rose, the impact of the afternoon finally hit me. There hadn't been time to have a proper emotional reaction at the scene. My mind had been occupied by the arrival of the police, the conversation with

24

Detective Rizzi, and my experience with Bobby Johnson, the *Post* reporter.

Now, in the welcome quiet of the living room, I began to tremble; my nerve ends were like exposed, sputtering electric wires. I went to the liquor cabinet and poured myself a larger snifter of Vaughan's favorite Blanton's Bourbon than I would have under ordinary circumstances. I took the drink to my bedroom, stripped off my clothes, put on a powder blue sweat suit I'd packed in case I had the energy and urge to walk laps in Manhattan (I hadn't), covered it with my robe, and returned to the living room where I sat in a chair that had unofficially become mine since arriving.

*   *   *

Waldo Morse had been born and raised in Cabot Cove. His family owned a small motel on the outskirts of town, which gave Waldo exposure to a wider variety of people than most other youngsters his age. Not that Morse's Blueberry Motel attracted a sophisticated group of world travelers. But interesting people had stayed there: some to fish the trout- and salmon-laden streams, many to enjoy the spectacular fall foliage, others just passing through on their way to other places.

Waldo was, as I recalled, a 'good boy.' He worked hard at the motel when he was old enough to shoulder some of the responsibility, and was an average student at Cabot Cove High School. He was best known for his exploits on the football field, an outstanding running back who'd been voted to the first-string all-Maine team his senior year.

Waldo attended a junior college for a year, maybe two, and stayed in Cabot Cove. He married a girl he'd dated in high school, and they quickly had two children. It wasn't easy for me to remember these details because I had never been a personal friend of Waldo and Nancy Morse. In fact, I only saw them once every couple of months in a store, or when passing in a car, and had virtually no firsthand knowledge of their life together. But there was the powerful Cabot Cove gossip mill that ensured that no one could ever live a truly private life there.

While taking marine biology courses in the junior college, Waldo had become fascinated with the sea and signed on as a hand on local lobster boats that left each morning from the town dock. Then, if memory serves, he bought his own lobster boat and moved south to picturesque, touristy Ogunquit, where I was told he became a relatively successful fisherman. It struck me as strange at the time because Nancy and the kids remained in Cabot Cove. His decision to move to Ogunquit had something to do, as I recall, with less competition there. But the real reason, according to more credible informants, was that Waldo and Nancy weren't getting along. That version proved out when the divorce came, evidently an amicable one because Waldo returned to Cabot Cove on a regular basis to visit his family.

While we kept up with Waldo Morse's life through the grapevine, one aspect of it suddenly became public knowledge, not only in Cabot Cove but in all of Maine, and undoubtedly beyond. He was arrested in Ogunquit and charged with drug smuggling.

According to newspaper accounts— embellished by those who claimed to have the 'straight scoop'—Waldo had allowed his lobster boat to be used by drug runners from the Caribbean and Florida. These dealers would place narcotics in watertight containers in Waldo's lobster traps—lobster 'cars'—to be picked up later by Waldo and delivered to other members of the drug ring somewhere in Maine. Most of the drugs ended up in Boston, said the reports, although that was never confirmed.

It was anticipated that Waldo would receive a stiff jail sentence. But a deal was struck. He turned state's evidence in return for immunity and a place in the Federal Witness Protection Program. The trial ended, the major figures were convicted and sentenced to long prison terms, and Waldo vanished.

That was the last I'd heard of him until that fateful afternoon on Fifth Avenue.

Waldo's wife, Nancy, was a clean-cut, rosy-cheeked, and energetic young blonde who'd been a popular cheerleader in high school. A good mother, it was said, and a woman who kept a low profile in Cabot Cove. After Waldo became a prosecution witness, there was natural and justifiable concern for the safety of Nancy and her children. But nothing happened to them, and those fears eventually dissipated.

Some of my friends speculated that because Waldo had lived in Ogunquit and was divorced, the drug dealers with whom he'd become involved never knew he had a family in Cabot Cove. If that was true, Nancy Morse and the kids were fortunate. From what I'd always heard, people involved in the drug world don't differentiate between women, children, and husband-informants.

Nancy and the kids stayed in Cabot Cove after Waldo's submersion into the famous but flawed witness protection program. The kids continued in school, and she ran her home and life quietly.

*　　　*　　　*

I suffered a sudden chill and walked to the center of the living room. Would the police know that Waldo had been in the witness protection program, and as a result simply bury him without notifying anyone?

What a horrible contemplation. Nancy Morse certainly should be made aware of her husband's demise. My shoulders felt heavy as I realized I might be the only person in a position to break that sorry news to her. But I resolved not to let that happen. I would call Detective Rizzi first thing in the morning and demand that an official notification of his death be delivered to the family. But then I wondered if notifying Nancy Morse that her husband had been murdered would place her and her children in jeopardy? How did the witness protection program work? Were the families of such individuals taken care of, informed of death, counseled, given some sort of insurance proceeds to help them continue with their lives? These questions, and many more, were gnawing at me when Vaughan Buckley turned his key in the door and stepped into the apartment.

'Jessica. I didn't think you'd be back so early.'

'I didn't think I would, either.'

He made himself a drink and settled across the coffee table from me. 'Oh, before I forget,' he said, pulling a scrap of paper from his shirt pocket. 'My secretary took this message for you. "Joe Charles. Tell Jessica Fletcher that Joe Charles will know."'

'What does it mean?' I asked.

Vaughan laughed. 'Beats me, but that's exactly what the message was. "Joe Charles. Tell Jessica Fletcher that Joe Charles will know."'

'Who left the message?'

'According to my secretary, the caller hung up without giving his name.'

Until then, I hadn't said anything to Vaughan about Waldo Morse. But I wanted to share it with someone. Because Vaughan sat in front of me, he became the obvious choice. I told him everything that had happened since first spotting Waldo.

'That's a remarkable story, Jess,' Vaughan said. 'You know nothing about his life after the trial ended?'

I shook my head. 'Nothing. Obviously, he ended up in New York, and at the time of his death was playing Santa Claus on the street.'

'It sounds like these people he turned in got even,' Vaughan said.

'That would seem the logical explanation, although I learned years ago to not always accept logical explanations, especially where murder is involved. My major concern is that his family be properly notified. Do you think the police will do that?'

'If they know who he is.'

'Exactly what I was thinking. Someone in the witness protection program would have false identity. I can't imagine Waldo carrying anything to indicate that he has a family back in Cabot Cove. In fact, I'd be surprised if he didn't take special steps to see that they were never linked to him.'

'What do you know about his family?' Vaughan asked.

'Not much. His wife and children are still there, but once Waldo left, he became an unknown person.'

'Any idea of his life here in New York, aside from playing Santa on a street corner?' Vaughan asked.

'No, but I think I have an obligation to find out.'

Vaughan smiled. 'You can't resist getting involved in this sort of thing, can you?'

'I don't think it's a matter of satisfying personal needs. But yes, I do have a certain fascination with murder. You and my readers should appreciate that.'

Vaughan stretched and stood. 'All I can say, Jess, is go slow and be careful. The witness protection program is a strange world, filled with bad people and even worse motives. Sure you just don't want to forget it, finish up promoting your book and head back to Cabot Cove to start your next one for us?'

I sighed. 'The idea is tempting, but I have to find out what happened. I won't burden you and Olga. Would you prefer that I move into a hotel? That would give me more freedom and . . .'

'Freedom? You make us sound like jailers. You can come and go as you please. If Olga and I can be of any help, including this Waldo Morse business, just yell. We're both very fond of you, Jess.'

The dogs, Sadie and Rose, came to my chair,

one on each side, and placed their chins on my lap. I rubbed them in the groove between their eyes.

'Looks like they're fond of you, too,' Vaughan said.

I stood and said, 'The look in Waldo's eyes the first time I saw him was like a frightened, tired dog that's been on the run for a long time. Thank you for being such a good friend, Vaughan. I think I'll take a bath and get dressed. We are having dinner out again, I assume. Not good for my commitment to a slimmer waistline.'

'Indulge yourself while you're here, Jess. Once you're back in Cabot Cove, you can diet all you want. When you're our guest in New York, indulgence is expected.'

I laughed. 'The problem is I'm about to indulge myself in investigating the murder of a former drug runner turned Santa Claus. While that might not put weight on me, it certainly weighs heavy. See you in an hour.'

CHAPTER SIX

We had dinner in a private room of a Japanese restaurant called Nippon. The presentation of the food was beautiful, and some of the dishes, especially something called *Sake Kawayaki*—smoked salmon skin soaked in sake and broiled to crisp perfection—were delicious to this pedestrian palate. But not to the extent of abandoning my love of lobster cookouts, homemade biscuits, corn-on-the-cob, and blueberry pie.

We sat on silk cushions on the floor (more suited to a younger person's vertebrae), and were joined around the black-lacquered table by another of Buckley House's authors, Harrison Libby, and his wife, Zelda. Mr Libby had written a book in which he traced the sexual lineage of four-legged animals to us two-legged species. He had flowing white hair, wore jeans and a sari, and was inordinately fond of four-letter words. Zelda claimed to be an interior decorator; her choice of makeup and clothing did little to instill in me any faith in her ability to create a harmonious setting. Still, it was an interesting evening, but could have ended sooner.

To be honest, the real problem with dinner was me. As hard as I tried to focus on what Libby and his wife were saying, I had trouble shifting gears and setting aside Waldo Morse for longer than minutes at a time. Had I not thought it rude, I would have taken out a pad and pencil, and made notes about how I intended to initiate my investigation. I just hoped that time and the sake would not cause me to forget what I'd been thinking during dinner. The minute I returned to the apartment, I went to my room and wrote down every thought I could resurrect.

Had it been earlier, I would have called my physician friend in Cabot Cove, Seth Hazlitt. The message Vaughan had given me, that someone named Joe Charles would know, intrigued me. I might not have thought anything of it except that the name rang a distant bell. For some reason I connected it with Cabot Cove, although I couldn't put my finger on why. Seth, who prided himself on remembering everything about the people of the town, might have a better recollection than mine. But I didn't want to awaken him. Most people in Cabot Cove go to bed early and get up even earlier. The call would have to wait until morning.

As far as I knew (and any knowledge I had was only hearsay), Waldo's wife and children had not been financially deprived by his entrance into the witness protection program. I'd heard from the mailman, local merchants, and others in Cabot Cove that they seemed to be quite comfortable. A large addition had been put on the house, a new cherry red Volvo station wagon and a black-and-gold Jeep Wrangler sat in the driveway, and the mailman regularly delivered videotapes, compact discs, and books from clubs to which Nancy belonged. Did the authorities who managed the witness protection program take especially good care of the families of people involved in it? That was one of the things I hoped to find out.

Where had Waldo lived in New York City? He'd played Santa Claus, which meant someone had to have hired him. But he'd likely used another name because of the need for his underground existence. What identification was on his person when he was shot? I should have asked, another question to raise with Detective Rizzi.

Had Waldo been in contact with his wife and children once he'd turned state's evidence? I wasn't aware that he had, although that didn't prove anything. Maybe there were channels through which people in his circumstances maintained a relationship with family. Nancy Morse would be the best source of information about that.

I thought of his parents, but recalled that both had died in a fire at the motel. It was now a fast-food outlet. My list was growing too long, each question leading to at least two others. I decided the best thing was a good night's sleep, provided my mind would indulge me that luxury.

I announced through a series of yawns that I was going to bed, but I'd taken only a few steps toward my room when the phone rang.

'At this hour?' Olga Buckley said.

Vaughan answered, listened intently, then glanced in my direction. 'It's for you, Jessica.'

Who would be calling me? Not many people knew I was there. I'd left the address and phone number with Seth and Morton Metzger in Cabot Cove, but there was no need for anyone else to have it because all my arrangements in New York were handled through Buckley House.

'Hello,' I said.

'Mrs Fletcher. Bobby Johnson from the *Post.*'

'How did you . . . ?' My prophecy had been fulfilled.

'Did you see the story?' he asked.

'What story?'

'About the Santa Claus murder. It's in the edition that just came out.'

'No, I have not seen it.'

'It wasn't easy getting a good photo of you, but I think the one we went with looks okay.'

'Photo? Of me? Why would you—how dare you run my picture.'

'Hey, Mrs Fletcher, I know a big one when I see it. There's no sense in us being on opposite sides in this thing. Play ball with me, and we'll both make out good.'

'I have nothing further to say until I see the story. Thank you for telling me about it.'

'My pleasure. By the way, I've done a little digging. Looks to me like it might have been a drug hit.'

I was speechless. Had he pierced the veil of secrecy surrounding Waldo? Did he know about the trial, about Waldo turning state's evidence, about having entered the witness protection program and disappearing for all

36

these years? If so, he was an even better reporter than I'd given him credit for. No, more than that. He was world-class.

It struck me that I could benefit from staying in touch with him, as unpleasant a contemplation as that was. I knew very little about New York City; he obviously knew a great deal. 'Mr Johnson,' I said, 'I'll look at the story, and then perhaps we can talk. How do I reach you?'

He gave me numbers at the *Post* and at home. 'Call any time, day or night, Mrs Fletcher. I swiped a copy of your latest novel from our book reviewer's desk. Looks like you're about to get a million dollars worth of publicity. Hope your publisher appreciates it.'

'I . . . good night, Mr Johnson.' I turned to Vaughan and Olga. 'That was a reporter from the *New York Post*,' I said. 'They've done a story about Waldo Morse's murder and used a picture of me.'

Vaughan put on his coat, 'I'll run out and get a copy,' he said. 'Be back in a few minutes.'

Ten minutes later he stood in the doorway holding up a copy of the paper. Most of the front page was taken up with the photograph of me. An insert in the lower right-hand corner was a picture of a very dead Santa Claus. The headline in large type read: 'SANTA DEAD.' A smaller headline beneath it said: 'DRUG DEALERS RUB OUT KRIS KRINGLE. XMAS CANCELED.'

Beneath my picture was the caption: '*Famed murder mystery writer Jessica Fletcher, who witnessed the slaughter on Fifth Avenue, is reported to have photographed the entire event and will devote her yuletide New York holiday to solving this brutal, distinctly unseasonable crime.*'

CHAPTER SEVEN

Once the initial shock of the *Post*'s front page had passed, I sat down with Vaughan and Olga to read the story that took up all of Page Three and jumped to another page deeper inside. Initially, I think, Vaughan found the situation somewhat amusing. But then when he read that I was staying with my publisher and his wife in their 'palatial' apartment in the Dakota, the bemused smile on his lips turned to a hard line. 'We'll be inundated with press and curiosity seekers,' he muttered.

'I'm sorry about this, Vaughan,' I said. 'I hope you know I didn't tell the reporter I was staying here.'

'Of course you didn't. The question is, how do we handle this?'

I said, 'I think I should move to a hotel.'

'What good will that do?' Olga asked. 'They'll find you wherever you go.'

'Yes, but the burden won't be on you.'

'Absolutely not,' Vaughan said. He paced the

large room. 'We'll gut this out together. Besides, as long as it's happened, we all have to admit it will help sell your book.'

I felt a twinge of resentment. He was right, of course, but I wished he hadn't seen it that way.

'I suggest we all try to get some sleep,' Olga said. 'Looks like it could be a busy day tomorrow.'

The phone rang.

'Or tonight,' Vaughan said, answering. It was a local radio station wanting to interview me. Vaughan cupped his hand over the mouthpiece and told me the nature of the call, his eyebrows arched into question marks. I shook my head. 'Sorry, Mrs Fletcher isn't available at the moment,' he said.

The phone rang again. And again. All media, and all wanting interviews with me.

'This is horrendous,' I said. 'I cannot subject you to this. Have your publicity people find me a secure hotel tomorrow.'

Olga protested again, but Vaughan held up his hand. 'Maybe Jessica is right, Olga. Not for our sake, of course, but she might feel better handling this in the impersonal atmosphere of a hotel suite. We'll talk about it in the morning.' He put on the answering machine, smiled smugly, and said, 'You can call them back tomorrow, Jess—if you choose to.'

I lay on my bed stiff as a board, eyes wide open, ears picking up the ring of the telephone and the faint sound of Vaughan's voice informing callers that the phone couldn't or wouldn't be answered at the moment. 'Leave your message after the beep and . . .'

I needed sleep. But when I was still awake at four the next morning, I gave up, clicked on the light next to the bed, and sat against the pink tufted headboard. Seth Hazlitt usually got up a little after five. He wouldn't be too upset— would he?—getting started an hour earlier. He answered on the first ring, the result of years of calls at odd hours from pregnant women about to deliver.

'Awful early to be callin', isn't it, Jess?'

'I know, and I apologize, but I had to. Seth, have you heard what happened to me yesterday?'

'Happened to you? Haven't heard a thing.'

'There hasn't been news there about the murder I witnessed?'

He was now fully awake. 'Run that by me again,' he said.

I told him as succinctly as possible what had happened to me on Fifth Avenue, and its aftermath. When I finished my capsulized tale, I was met with silence. 'Seth? Are you there?'

'Ayuh, I'm here. Waldo Morse? Sure, I remember him. I remember even better him gettin' involved with drug pushers from down south. You sure it was him?'

'Positive.'

'You say they claim you took pictures of it?'

40

'Yes. Because I did. I have the roll of film in my camera.'

He groaned. 'Don't talk about things like that on the phone, Jess. You should know better.'

'You asked, Seth and . . .'

'Let's get off that subject,' he said. 'What do you want me to do?'

'Nothing. No, not true. I received a mysterious message. It came through my publisher. The caller, who didn't give his name, said that Joe Charles would know.'

'Know what?'

'I don't know, but the name is familiar. Maybe it has something to do with Waldo's murder. Maybe not. Does the name Joe Charles mean anything to you?'

'Nope, but I'll give it some good thought once I'm showered and garbed up. Got plenty of time to do that this particular mornin'.'

I didn't apologize again because there was an unmistakable chuckle in his voice. I said, 'I really would appreciate that, Seth. I'll be out all morning, but I'll be back here this afternoon. I might check into a hotel.'

'Don't do that, Jess. Better to be with friends at a time like this.'

'Yes, I know but . . .'

'You listen to me, Jessica Fletcher. I've never steered you wrong. You stay away from those New York City hotels. Heah?'

I smiled. 'Yes, I hear. I'm signing books this

41

morning at a store that specializes in murder mysteries, and I have a radio interview at eleven. I don't think I have a lunch appointment, so I'll be back here at noon, maybe a little later. If you come up with anything about Joe Charles, call me. If you get the answering machine, leave a message and I'll get back to you.'

'I hate those answering machines, and you know it. I always hang up on 'em.'

'Don't hang up on this one. Thank you, Seth. You're a dear.'

Talking to him had a medicinal effect on me. I quickly fell asleep, only to be awakened at six by Olga's rap on my door. I wasn't due at the store until nine-thirty. 'Sorry to get you up so early, Jess, but the number of calls that came in during the night is overwhelming. The doorman says there are at least thirty members of the press downstairs and an even bigger crowd watching them.'

'Oh, goodness, what have I gotten me—and you—into?'

She smiled broadly. 'Don't worry about it. Things were getting dull around here anyway. Come, have some breakfast.'

The limousine provided by Buckley House was waiting in front of the Dakota. Ruth Lazzara, more ebullient than she'd been on the previous day—if that were possible—sat inside. On her lap were a half-dozen copies of the *Post*. She said before I even had a chance to fully

42

enter the limo, 'Fantastic! You are amazing, Mrs Fletcher.'

'I didn't do anything except have the misfortune of witnessing a murder.'

'But how perfect. The world's most famous mystery writer being the key witness in a sensational killing.'

I wanted to debate the issue but decided not to bother. Each person has his or her private prism through which events are refracted. This young woman was charged by her publisher with getting maximum publicity for its authors. The fact that this bonanza was the result of a tragic circumstance meant little. As the old saying goes, 'Say what you want, but spell my name right.'

If I'd been impressed by the line of people waiting for my previous book signing, this morning's crowd was staggering. Hundreds of people milled about outside Dastardly Acts, a small bookstore specializing in books about murder and other antisocial behavior. Joining them was a caravan of media vehicles that followed us from the Dakota, including a car containing the *Post* reporter who had started all the hoopla, Bobby Johnson. He'd shaved, and wore a suit and tie this morning. His celebrity status had obviously risen along with mine.

Ruth and I were ushered into the store by the owner, Winston Whitlock, and two uniformed private security guards. Once safely inside, Mr Whitlock, a tall, skeletal man with white hair and gray cheeks, and wearing a string tie whose clip was a copper disc on which was etched 'MURDER PAYS,' said anxiously, 'I'm afraid we're going to have to cancel this, Mrs Fletcher. The crowd is too big. There's no way we can assure your safety and the security of our customers.'

'I hope you realize this was not my intention,' I said. 'I looked forward to a quiet book signing in this lovely shop.'

'I know, but that's all a thing of the past.'

Ruth said, 'Why cancel? This is the best thing that could ever happen to this store. How many copies of Mrs Fletcher's new book do you have?'

The manager shrugged. 'Fifty, I think.'

'Where's the phone?' Ruth asked. Whitlock pointed to his desk. She dialed a number and said in a semi-hysterical voice, 'We need two hundred copies of Fletcher's book for the signing at Dastardly Acts. Get a messenger. Bring them yourself. Just get them here.'

'I think Mr Whitlock is right,' I said.

Ruth hung up. 'I'll make that decision, Mrs Fletcher.' Before I could respond, she said to Whitlock, 'If you're concerned about security, hire more guards. Buckley House will pay for them.'

Whitlock looked at me in confusion, then told an assistant to call the security firm and order more men.

'Perhaps I should just leave and . . .'

Ruth responded by taking my elbow and moving me to a table that had been set up for the autographing. 'Why don't you just sit down, Mrs Fletcher, and start signing books.'

My expression reminded her that I didn't sign books ahead of time. 'All right, sit and make yourself comfortable.' To the manager, she said, 'Could you get Mrs Fletcher coffee, maybe some Danish.'

I said I wasn't hungry.

One of the guards stationed at the front door came to where Whitlock was perched on the edge of the table next to me. 'Sir, the police are here.'

'I don't want any trouble,' Whitlock said, his voice flighty, his hands flapping in the air as though he wanted to fly south.

'It's a detective named Rizzi. He wants to talk to Mrs Fletcher.'

I looked up at him. 'Detective Rizzi. I intended to speak with him today. This would be as good a time as any.'

The guard ignored my words and looked to the man who was paying him. 'Let him in,' Whitlock said, abject despair in his voice.

Rizzi came through the door with another man, a much taller and more corpulent detective wearing a green raincoat. I stood. 'Good morning, Detective Rizzi.'

'Good morning, Mrs Fletcher. This is Detective Ryan.'

'Good morning to you, Detective Ryan.

45

Would you like coffee?'

Ms Lazzara interjected, looking at her watch, 'Could we make this quick? We're due to start autographing in ten minutes.'

'Who are you?' Rizzi asked.

'This is Ms Lazzara. She's in charge of publicity for my new book.'

'Yeah, well, I don't think there's going to be any autographing today.' Rizzi looked directly at me. 'Mrs Fletcher, we want you to come downtown with us.'

'I intended to do that later in the day. I have a number of questions I'd like answered.'

Rizzi and Ryan looked at each other. '*You* have questions to ask *us*. I think it's the other way around, Mrs Fletcher. You're a material witness to a murder.'

I suppose my face mirrored everything I was thinking. His expression didn't change, however, nor did that of his colleague. I said haughtily, 'I am well aware that I was a witness to a murder. I came forward, which is more than I can say for anyone else who was there. I actually had to pursue you in order to give you my name and where I was staying. You were totally disinterested. Now you come in here and announce to me that I am a material witness, as though you had to track me down. Are you about to arrest me?'

Rizzi winced. 'Calm down, Mrs Fletcher. It was a busy day, people getting zipped all over town. Anyway, I didn't know who you were. I don't read much, but my wife, Emily, reads all the time. She saw the *Post* story and got excited. She says you're one of the best mystery writers in the world.'

'That's flattering, Detective, but I don't know what it has to do with your change in attitude about my being a witness.'

'It has nothing to do with it. Just come with us.'

I shrugged at Ruth and Whitlock.

'The signing will only take an hour,' Ruth said. 'Surely, you can allow her that.'

'I got my orders,' Rizzi said.

I said to the others, 'Sorry, but I think I have to go with the gentlemen.'

'This is outrageous!' Ruth said. 'Give me your name and badge number.'

Rizzi winced again, an expression I was to see often over the ensuing days. 'You, too?' he said to Ruth. He mumbled his name and number.

As I started to put on my coat, Rizzi said, 'Before we go, maybe you could sign one of your books to Emily. Make it to Emily and her mother, Mrs Wilson.'

'The nerve,' Ruth said.

'You certainly do have a different approach to things, Detective,' I said, picking up a copy of my book, opening it, and writing: 'To Emily and Mrs Wilson.' Under it I scribbled, 'It must be very exciting having a New York City detective in the family.' I signed and handed it

47

to him. He muttered a form of thanks and led me from the store.

The crowds had swelled outside. Bobby Johnson, the *Post* reporter, was right up front. 'Mrs Fletcher. Where are you going?' he yelled.

'To police headquarters, I think I'm being detained, if not arrested.' I added, 'Thanks to you and your story.'

Johnson ignored my comment and asked the detectives where they were taking me. They didn't answer. Ryan held open the back door of an unmarked car.

Ruth came running from the store and shouted, 'Don't forget the interview at eleven.' She shoved a piece of paper with the address of the radio station through the partially opened rear window. I dropped it to the floor. Somehow, I knew that particular radio show would be minus one guest that morning. Hopefully, the host was comfortable with soliloquizing.

CHAPTER EIGHT

The few individuals who end up in Morton Metzger's Cabot Cove police headquarters are usually impressed with how clean and cheerful it is. Of course, it doesn't get a great deal of use—an occasional drunk given a cell in which to sleep it off, an out-of-state motorist speeding through town and demonstrating too much big-city bravado for Morton's taste, or occasionally someone who's committed a more serious crime like poaching blueberries. Or murder.

The police headquarters to which I was taken by detectives Rizzi and Ryan looked as though it had been created by a Hollywood set designer for a documentary on poverty. Pea green walls hadn't been painted in years, and what paint was left hung in flaky sheets. The furniture was battered and scarred, and the windows were dirty to the extent that I couldn't see through them. A heavy, pungent cloud of tobacco, body odor, and urine hung palpably over everything. Most disconcerting, at least for me, was the noise level. Back home, Sheriff Metzger plays tapes he's made from his collection of Kostelanetz and Montovani recordings, which he claims is the largest in Maine. But there was no music in this New York City precinct. Dozens of people milled about, all yelling at each other. A long wooden bench was crammed with men and women under arrest and waiting to be processed. They looked as though the predicament wasn't new to them or, in some cases, even unpleasant.

I wished I were somewhere else.

'Come on, Mrs Fletcher, we can talk better in one of the interview rooms.'

Interview? Interesting genteel euphemism for interrogation, or grilling. No matter. I was relieved to enter the room and have the door close behind me; the outside din was muffled by half.

'Have a seat, Mrs Fletcher,' Rizzi said. He picked up the phone and said, 'Get in here!' Minutes later a young female uniformed officer appeared carrying a courtroom stenographer's machine. She didn't acknowledge me, nor I her.

'Make yourself at home,' Rizzi said to me.

Make myself at home, I thought. Not easy to do in such surroundings. I pulled out a wooden chair with one arm missing and sat in it. It was uncomfortable not because the arm was missing, or because the seat was hard, but because it seemed to lean forward. 'I think the legs on this chair are broken,' I said.

Rizzi uttered what might be characterized as a laugh. 'The front legs are cut off an inch, Mrs Fletcher. Keeps suspects leaning forward and off-balance.'

'Am I sitting in this chair because I am a suspect?' I asked.

'You didn't whack Santa Claus.'

'You're quite right, Detective Rizzi. I did not "whack" Santa Claus. Now, could we get to the point of bringing me here? I intended to call you today and arrange for a time to meet, but you usurped that prerogative.'

'Whatever you say, Mrs Fletcher.' Rizzi sat in his own shaky chair across the table from me. 'Let's see the pictures.'

'Pardon?'

50

'The pictures, Mrs Fletcher. I can read. The *Post* says you took pictures of the murder. I'd like to have them.' I started to say something but he quickly added, 'Strike that, Mrs Fletcher. I want them.'

He sounded like he meant it. I still didn't want to turn over the roll of film until I'd had a chance to have it developed, which I intended to do that day. I'd pushed a little button on my camera that allowed me to rewind the film before the roll was finished and had placed it in my purse. I smiled. 'Detective Rizzi, I'm surprised that someone in your position would believe everything they read in the press, especially a paper like the *Post*.'

'Nothin' wrong with the *Post*, Mrs Fletcher. I suppose you're the *Times* and *Wall Street Journal* type.'

'I read those papers, but I wouldn't classify myself as a "type."' I waited. The stenographer looked up and waited, too. Rizzi was slumped in his chair, his chin on his breastbone, his dark eyes looking at me from beneath heavy brows. He said in a gruff voice without raising his chin, 'Mrs Fletcher, *finita la commedia*.'

'I don't know what that means,' I said.

'It means the game is up. The farce is over. You don't speak Italian?'

'No, I don't.'

'Yeah, well, I forget a lot of it because I'm not married to an Italian woman, but when I visit my mother, she talks Italian and some of it

51

sticks. By the way, thanks for the book for Emily. She'll really appreciate it, probably send you a note. She likes writing notes to people.'

'That's a nice trait.'

'Yeah, I suppose it is. The film, Mrs Fletcher. Where is it?'

While the sparring had been almost enjoyable, I also knew that the time for bantering was over. As much as I wanted to have the film developed myself, I decided I was asking for big trouble by continuing to withhold it. 'All right,' I said. 'I never intended to not give you the prints. I wanted a chance to see them first. Obviously, I won't be able to do that.' I opened my purse and reached in. The roll of film did not immediately fall under my fingers, and I began to rummage. When that didn't produce a result, I opened the bag wide and used my eyes, as well as my fingers. Nothing. It wasn't there.

'Something wrong, Mrs Fletcher?'

'Yes. I put the film in this purse last night. It seems to be missing.'

'Missing? What did it do, develop itself and take a walk?'

'No, I don't think it did that. I can't explain it, but I did take the roll of film from my camera last night and put it in this purse. I could not be mistaken about that.'

He narrowed his eyes and snorted.

I shrugged and extended my hands. 'I'm not lying to you. The film was here. Now it isn't,

52

and I am as distressed as you are.'

'Don't count on it, Mrs Fletcher. This is a serious matter. I could charge you with withholding state's evidence.'

'But I didn't do anything with the evidence. I'm trying to be cooperative, but the film simply isn't here.'

He expelled an impatient, exaggerated sigh. 'Okay, Mrs Fletcher, we'll skip the photographs for now and get a statement from you about what you saw yesterday.'

My personal debate over telling the police of what I knew about Waldo Morse now turned into an internal shouting match. I was on thin ice and knew it. Rizzi had been pleasant enough, but I didn't harbor any illusions that he couldn't—wouldn't—turn tougher if he thought I was playing games. I had to be honest.

'Detective Rizzi, I knew the man in the Santa Claus costume who was killed.'

I'd gotten his attention. He sat up straight, leaned forward, elbows on the table, and opened his eyes wide. 'Is that so, Mrs Fletcher? Suppose you tell me more about that.'

It was my turn to sigh. I sat back as best I could and collected my thoughts. 'The victim's name was Waldo Morse.'

'Morse? That's not what his ID said.'

'No, I'm sure it didn't. You see, Waldo Morse grew up in Cabot Cove, the town in Maine where I've lived for a long time. He was a lobster fisherman in Ogunquit until he was accused of using his boat to help smuggle drugs into New England. He became a witness for federal authorities in return for being taken into the witness protection program. I hadn't seen or heard of him since that happened, which is at least ten years ago. Then, as I was walking down Fifth Avenue, I thought I recognized the Santa Claus. I was right. It was Waldo. What name was he carrying on his identification?'

'Mrs Fletcher, *you* just keep answering *my* questions.'

I stiffened. 'I don't you see why this should be a one-way street,' I said. 'I think I have a right to ask questions of my own.'

I detected a slight smile on the stenographer's lips, and was glad Rizzi hadn't. His response was slow in coming. 'Mrs Fletcher, you seem like a very nice lady, and I know you're a famous writer and all that. You're probably down here in New York having a good time publicizing your new book, and you probably look at guys like me as though we're dirtbags.'

'Dirtbags?'

'Yeah. Maybe not as good as you and the people you hang out with. Emily, my wife, sometimes sees me that way. She's a WASP. She grew up in Jersey where the worst thing ever happened was the garbage man didn't put the cover back on the can. She meets me, an

54

Italian from Brooklyn, and falls in love because she never met an Italian from Brooklyn before. All she knew were wimpy guys from Jersey. My mother-in-law, Mrs Wilson, looks at me funny, too.'

'I don't know why she would,' I said, wanting to make him feel better. 'Do you always call your mother-in-law Mrs Wilson?'

'Yeah. She told me to. She went along with the marriage because she didn't have a choice, but she told me to always call her Mrs Wilson.'

'You don't sound especially fond of her,' I said.

'What's to be fond of? She looks down her nose at everybody, especially me, but I have to put up with it. I mean, she is my wife's mother.'

'Why are you telling me this?'

He stood, his face hard. 'Just to let you know, Mrs Fletcher, that I'm not what you probably think I am. I know a lot about a lot of things. I know my wines, and I spend a lot of time in museums. You know much about art? You ever hear of Domenikos Theotokopoulos?' He didn't give me a chance to say that I hadn't. 'That was El Greco's real name. I like Matisse and Chagall, but I never did like the Cubists. What's your favorite wine?' Again, no time for an answer. 'I prefer the softer Burgundies of the cotes de Beaune, and I find a Puligny Montrachet satisfying at certain times.'

'Of course,' I said.

'You see, Mrs Fletcher, people like you and

Mrs Wilson underestimate people like me, which can be good because it gives me an edge.'

I looked into his black eyes and tried to fathom the psychology behind what he was saying. He was obviously a man who felt there were two worlds—his, and a much larger one made up of people who scorned him. Sad, I thought. I also reminded myself that what he'd said was undoubtedly true. He was a man who always looked for the edge and used it, especially with people 'like me.'

'So you knew this Waldo Morse. Did you talk to him? Before he was killed, I mean.'

'Yes. The day before.'

'The day before?'

'That's when I first recognized and approached him. He told me to come back the next day at two. I did, and he was murdered. That's why I was there and saw it happen.'

'Did you talk to him yesterday, just before he was shot?'

I shook my head.

'What did you talk about the day before?'

'Nothing.' I looked across the table at a stone-faced Rizzi, and my resolve waned. I drew a breath and said, 'Again, may I ask what name he was carrying.'

'No. Witness protection program? You say this guy was in it?'

'That's my understanding.'

'We'll check the Feds on that. What else can you tell me?'

I pursed my lips. 'Nothing. Is there anything further you can tell me, Detective Rizzi?' I glanced at the stenographer.

'You're going to be in New York for a while?' Rizzi asked.

'Yes. Through New Year's Eve.'

'Good. Tell you what, Mrs Fletcher. You go on promoting your book, and I'll go on trying to solve this murder. Give me a call now and then. If I think it's okay, I'll tell you how I'm doing. Fair enough?'

'I suppose it has to be. Am I free to go?'

'You were always free to go. I didn't cuff you, did I?'

'You also didn't tell me I didn't have to come with you this morning. I'm afraid there are a lot of people at that bookstore who have been disappointed. So is a radio talk show host who's sitting in his studio at this moment reading from the Manhattan phone book.' Rizzi's expression said that if anything in this world concerned him, disappointed book buyers and radio hosts were not on the list.

He escorted me from the room. As we passed through the squad room, he was stopped by a uniformed officer who said, 'You got a call, Al. It's the Feds about the Marsh case.'

Marsh? Feds? Could he be talking about Waldo Morse, who'd perhaps changed his name to Marsh? I would have assumed that anyone in a witness protection program would go further afield in choosing a new name—Symington, or Wolinoski, or Buttafucco—but that represented only my logic.

Marsh. I kept that name with me as Rizzi took me to the door. I extended my hand; he took it with uncertainty. 'I hope your wife enjoys the book, Detective Rizzi.'

'She will. Thanks.'

'And Mrs Wilson, too. Have a nice day.'

'It'll be a lot nicer when you find that film.'

It had grown sharply colder. I looked up into a low sky the color of lead and pulled my coat collar up around my neck to shield against a brisk wind. It looked, and smelled, like snow.

The film!

Who could have taken the roll of film?

Vaughan or Olga Buckley? No.

Their housekeeper, Gina? Unlikely.

Someone at Dastardly Acts? Possibly.

But why?

Maybe it fell out of my purse when leaving the bookstore.

Maybe . . . maybe lots of things.

I reached the corner and looked down at a homeless man who'd established himself on a grate. He'd spread out cardboard and had wrapped himself in a heavy blanket, his possessions in shopping bags at his side. He looked up and extended a hand. 'Just money to eat, lady. I don't drink.'

As I handed him a dollar bill, I was able to look closely at his face. What I saw were Waldo

Morse's eyes—frightened, defeated, life drained from them.

Poor man, I thought as I spotted a cab discharging a passenger a half block away. I ran for it and said to the driver through the open back door, 'I'm going to the Dakota apartments.'

He barked that he was off-duty and told me to close the door. I did and he drove off, leaving me with a distinctly bitter taste in my mouth. It wasn't so much from tasting too many plates of New York taxi drivers. I could deal with that, as unpleasant as it might be.

It was the death of Waldo Morse that was upsetting me.

I knew one thing for certain.

I had to find out the real story.

CHAPTER NINE

The press was camped outside the Dakota when I arrived. I waved off their questions and went to the apartment where Gina polished silver.

'Did the Buckleys leave messages for me?' I asked.

'Sí,' she said, handing me a yellow ruled legal pad containing a number of entries. The one I immediately responded to was a call from Seth Hazlitt.

'Where have you been?' he asked.

'Where I said I was going to be, at the—no, that isn't true. My appearances at the bookstore and the radio interview were canceled. I've been with the police.'

'I already know that, Jessica. The all-news station from Bangor just ran an item sayin' you'd been arrested.'

'I wasn't arrested, Seth. They just wanted to ask me some questions.'

'Where are you now?'

'Back at the apartment. I'm fine. The police were very nice to me.'

'If you say so. Looks like your memory is pretty good, Jess.'

'What do you mean?'

'Rememberin' the name Joe Charles. He's a local boy.'

'He is?'

'Ayuh, except Joe Charles wasn't his name when he was growin' up here. He's Flo Johnson's boy from up north of town. Called him Junior. Remember?'

'Flo Johnson. Yes, I do remember she had a son they called Junior. Junior Johnson. That's Joe Charles?'

'Sure is.'

'But why would the name Joe Charles ring a bell if I knew him as Junior Johnson?'

''Cause when he became a musician, he changed his name to Joe Charles. He had a band that used to work in these parts.'

60

'Now I remember. Is he still in Cabot Cove?'

'Nope. Not much work for a musician here, so seems he headed for the big city, Los Angeles first. His mother says he ended up in New York.'

'As a musician? Performing under the name Joe Charles?'

'She isn't certain about that. Seems the boy doesn't have much contact with her. Just like young people these days, leave your roots and forget they're still planted. Not hard to pick up a phone, drop a postcard to your mother once in a while. At any rate, Jess, he might be the same Joe Charles that came over your answering machine.'

'Seth, this has been extremely helpful. Anything else?'

'Nope, 'cept Mort got a nice letter from Parker Brothers this mornin' 'bout his board game. Seems like they're interested.'

'That's wonderful. He must be thrilled.'

'Not so's you'd notice.'

Our sheriff had been working on a murder mystery board game for years. Every time he thought he had it ready to submit, one of us would come up with another flaw and he'd start over. Two months ago he decided he'd made enough changes and announced he was sending it off to Parker Brothers.

'I have to run, Seth. Lots to do. Thanks again.'

'If I was you, Jessica Fletcher, I'd pack my

bags and come back home. New York City's bad enough without you witnessin' murders and endin' up a news item on the radio like some common criminal.'

'You know something, Seth, I just might do that. But not right away. Plans still proceeding for the New Year's Eve party?'

'Sure are. The only thing lackin' will be Jessica Fletcher. You think about what I said.'

'I promise I will. Congratulate Mort for me.'

I perused other messages on the page. Three were from Ruth Lazzara asking me to call the minute I returned. There were calls from media, including a London tabloid anxious to interview me because I'd been involved there a year ago investigating the murder of a dear friend, the *grande dame* of mystery writing, Marjorie Ainsworth.

I called Ruth Lazzara. Her assistant told me there had been a change in schedule that afternoon. Originally, there were only two interviews, one with *Publishers Weekly*, the 'Bible' of the publishing industry, the other with the *Village Voice*. Now, they'd sandwiched in four more.

'Impossible,' I told her. 'I made it clear that I need some time for myself during this trip. I don't want to be uncooperative but . . .'

'I'll have Ms Lazzara call you.'

Did I dare skip out? Obviously, I would honor the two interviews that had originally been arranged, but if I didn't know the specifics of the others, I couldn't very well show up.

I put on my coat and headed for the door. 'Please tell the Buckleys I'll be back sometime this evening, Gina, but not to plan on me for dinner.'

'*Sí*, Mrs Fletcher.'

I heard the phone ring and paused at the door to listen to the incoming message. It was Ruth Lazzara. She sounded positively frantic.

My *Publishers Weekly* interview was at three, and the *Village Voice* reporter was to meet me at Buckley House at six. They could count on me. The others could wait.

There was something else I had to do.

*   *   *

Local 802, the New York office of the American Federation of Musicians, was located far west on Forty-second Street. There was a lot of activity in a large room at the end of a hallway. A hundred people, musicians I assumed, milled about in what appeared to be a shape-up hall. I scanned the crowd for someone who looked official, and who might direct me to member records. Before I succeeded, a paunchy little man wearing a shirt opened to his belly, and sporting Fort Knox around his neck and on his fingers came up to me. 'You a singer?' he asked.

'Me? Heavens, no.'

'You sure you don't sing. I need a singer

63

tonight at Roseland.'

'I'm afraid I'm no singer. Only in the shower, and pretty bad at that.'

'You got a costume? Play maracas, cowbell?'

'Excuse me,' I said, walking to a desk in the corner at which a sullen gentleman sat. 'Excuse me, sir, I'm trying to locate a musician.'

'You come to the right place.' He grinned and took in the men and women on the floor with outstretched arms.

'I don't want to *hire* a musician. I'm trying to locate a certain individual. Where would member records be?'

'Upstairs.'

The woman in charge of member records was middle-aged and pleasant. I told her I was anxious to contact a musician who worked under the name Joe Charles.

'Why do you want to find him?' she asked.

She was obviously concerned I might be a process server, or from a collection agency. 'Nothing bad, I can assure you,' I said. 'He comes from my hometown in Maine. I have good news for him.'

That seemed to satisfy her. She went to a large bank of file drawers, pulled out a folder, and returned to her desk. 'Let's see,' she said. 'Yes. Joe Charles is a paid-up member.' She placed the folder in front of me. I took the address and phone number from it, thanked her, and left the building, my heart pounding. Things had worked quickly and smoothly. Here

64

I was with the address and phone number of the person I assumed had been referred to me by my mystery caller. Good old Seth. He'd really come through for me, as he usually did.

Junior Johnson, a.k.a. Joe Charles, lived on Crosby Street, of which I'd never heard. I had no idea where in Manhattan it was, but assumed cab drivers would know. I was wrong. The first two drivers shook their heads and said they didn't know any Crosby Street. I suggested to the second that he consult his map: 'No map, no map,' he said, speeding off. I was luckier with the third, an older man who was nicely dressed, and who actually seemed to display pride in being a taxi driver who knew his city.

'Not a very nice neighborhood you're going to,' he said, activating the meter.

'It won't be a problem in daylight, will it?'

'No, but it's not my favorite part of New York. Just keep your eyes open.'

I sat back in his refreshingly clean cab and watched the city slide by. It had started to snow. Fine, delicate flakes swirled about the windows and gave me a sense of security. Maybe that's why they call it a blanket of snow. I've always liked it when it snows in Cabot Cove. I love the crackling wood and aroma from the fireplace, the crunch beneath my feet when I walk outside, the pristine tranquility it drapes over the town. Would it snow enough to accomplish the same thing for me in Manhattan? I'd never been in New York City when it snowed. Another life experience.

We stopped for a light at the intersection of Bowery and Houston streets where two disheveled men rubbed dirty rags on the windshield despite my driver's attempts to wave them away. Another man, tottering from alcohol, knocked on my window and shook a paper cup at me.

'Sorry about that, ma'am,' the driver said as the light changed and he pulled away.

'I feel sorry for them,' I said. 'I was thinking how pleased I was to see the snow, but I'm sure they aren't happy about it.'

We pulled up in front of a beautiful old office building at the north end of Crosby Street, at the corner of Bleecker. I said to the driver, 'What unusual architecture.'

He replied, 'I'm really not up on architecture, ma'am, but I do know this building was designed by someone named Louis Sullivan. Pretty famous in his day.'

'I feel better already,' I said.

'Why?'

'I know this isn't a very nice neighborhood, but if a lovely building like this can survive here, it can't be all bad.'

He drove off, leaving me to admire the twelve-story building with its terracotta leafy designs that drew the eye to six angels above the cornice, their wings outspread as though to welcome visitors.

The address I'd been given at the musicians

union was two doors up from the office building. It looked like a warehouse or factory. Why would someone live in a factory? I wondered. I heard music coming from inside—dissonant, loud, grating electronic sounds that had the quality of long fingernails dragged across a blackboard.

I went up a few steps and stood at the front door, which was slightly ajar. Doorbells had been attached to the side of the door but the wires connecting them had been cut and dangled free.

I looked back at the street. The delicate flakes had turned fatter and wetter, which usually meant to us in Maine that the snowfall would not continue as long as if the flakes remained small and dry. But maybe rules of nature like that didn't apply in New York City. I pushed open the door and stepped into a large foyer. The walls were covered with graffiti, much of it patently offensive. The music was louder now, and came from above.

Startled by the sound of heavy shoes on a metal staircase, I looked up and saw a young man round the corner and continue toward me. He wore high military boots, shorts, and a purple-and-yellow Day-Glo tank top. His long hair was tied in a ponytail.

'Excuse me,' I said. He stopped. 'I'm looking for an old friend of mine, a musician named Joe Charles.'

'Upstairs, third floor. His name is on the

door.' He turned and was gone. Shorts in this weather? Maybe I was missing something.

I slowly ascended the stairs, my heels clanging on the metal with each step. As I got higher, the volume of the music increased. It came from behind the door on which 'JOE CHARLES' had been scribbled on a piece of cardboard. I'd never heard such music before. I call it music because the alternative was to label it 'sounds from a construction site.'

I knocked. Whoever was inside certainly wouldn't hear me above the level of the music. This time, I banged on the door with the fleshy portion of my hand. The music stopped. 'Who is it?' a man yelled.

'A friend of Waldo Morse,' I shouted back.

Although I couldn't see inside the room, I had the feeling that the person in it, presumably Joe Charles, was debating whether to respond. I waited what I thought was an appropriate amount of time, then raised my hand again and was prepared to knock when the door opened. Facing me was a short, chubby young man, but old enough to have seen much of his hair recede. His round face was covered with stubble, and his pale blue eyes had a watery quality to them. He wore coveralls over a bare torso. Rubber thongs were on feet in need of a bath.

'I'm sorry to interrupt your practice,' I said pleasantly, 'but I came here about something pretty important. My name is Jessica Fletcher.

68

I'm from Cabot Cove, Maine, and . . .'

'Sure, the mystery writer. My mother knew you, didn't she?'

'Mrs Johnson? Yes, I know your mother. Not well, but I certainly remember that she had a son everyone called "Junior," and who became quite a musician under the name Joe Charles. That is you, isn't it?'

He nodded. 'You said you were a friend of Waldo Morse. Why did you say that?'

'Well, I might not have been a close friend, but I was a witness to his murder. You probably read about that in the paper.'

He shook his head. 'I don't read the papers. Maybe *Rolling Stone, Downbeat.* Sure, I heard what happened to Waldo. A real bummer.'

I raised my eyebrows. 'Yes, I suppose it was a bummer, as you say. May I come in?'

He'd been cordial, but there was now conflict written on his face. 'I promise I won't take much of your time,' I said, 'but it is important that I speak with you.'

He stepped back to allow me to enter.

The room was very large; furniture was obviously not on the list of priorities. A mattress with a flowered sheet was on the floor in one corner. His clothing, what there was of it, hung from hooks along a wall. The kitchen was part of the main room, a small sink, stove and refrigerator tucked into a corner. There was a door which, I assumed, led to the bathroom. All of this was contained in the north end of the room.

The southern end was chockablock with musical instruments. There was a rack on which four keyboards of different sizes were mounted. A set of drums sat in a corner. A large instrument that appeared to be a marimba stood in front of the drums. Another rack, from which bells, tubes, and wooden sticks dangled, was in the center of the area. A computer completed the paraphernalia.

'I've never seen so many instruments in one place,' I said.

'I use them all sometimes.'

'Do you use them outside of the apartment? You must need a truck to take them to work.'

'Sometimes. I have a couple of groupies who help me.'

'Groupies? Women who follow you around?'

He smiled. 'Yeah. Fem Lib at work. As long as they're going to hang around, they might as well make themselves useful.'

'That's pragmatic,' I said. I looked around the room. 'May I sit down?'

'Okay.' He pointed to a black hydraulic chair in front of the rack of keyboards, pulled a plastic milk crate from the kitchen, and sat on it, facing me. 'Who told you about me?' he asked.

'I don't know. That sounds silly. Someone left an anonymous message with my publisher in which you were mentioned. I checked friends back home, and they reminded me about you. The message said you would know.'

'Know what?'

'I don't know. That's why I'm here. I must admit, I'm very confused about Waldo. I remember when he got into all that trouble in Cabot Cove.'

'Ogunquit,' Charles corrected me.

'Yes. Ogunquit. Have you been in touch with Waldo since he went into the witness protection program?'

'A little. Not much.'

'Had he been in New York City all this time?'

A shake of the head. 'No, Waldo was relocated—I think that's what they call it—he was relocated out in Colorado.'

'Did you know him when he was there?'

'I knew him from Cabot Cove, Mrs Fletcher.'

'Of course. You lost all contact with Waldo while he was in Colorado?'

'Yup. We were never real good friends in Maine. We hung around a little together. I was into music, he was a football player, but we got along. I remember the last conversation I had with him there. He told me he was marrying Nancy. I told him I thought he was nuts.'

'Nuts? To marry Nancy?'

'To marry anybody. He was a young guy. I felt trapped in Cabot Cove and couldn't wait to get out, but he seemed to want to keep himself in that trap, get married, have kids, try to make

71

a living there.'

'So you went to Los Angeles to find fame and fortune.'

It was a gentle, self-effacing laugh. 'I'm afraid I didn't find much of that in L.A. Kind of ironic, Mrs Fletcher. I gave Waldo a lecture about staying single, but six months after I get to L.A., I meet a chick and marry her. It lasted almost a year.'

'I'm sorry.'

'No big deal. We didn't have any kids, so when we split, nobody got hurt. She was okay. I still talk to her once in a while if she's in New York, or I make it out to the West Coast.'

I stopped asking questions and glanced toward windows that overlooked Crosby Street. It was snowing harder now; a strong wind rattled the panes.

'Want a cup of coffee or something?' he asked.

'That would be lovely. I prefer tea.'

'I have to go get it. Only be a minute.'

'Please, don't bother. I thought you had it here.'

'There's a Korean deli up the street. Want something to eat? A donut? Candy bar?'

'No, thank you. Just tea will be fine. A little milk.' I watched him put on a green army surplus overcoat that reached his ankles, and a black stocking cap. 'Can I buy?' I asked.

'If you want to. I'm a little short of cash. I have a gig tomorrow night.'

I handed him a five-dollar bill. He thanked me, left, and I heard the sound of his feet on the metal stairs.

I stood and surveyed the room with more scrutiny than when I'd first entered. Junior Johnson, alias Joe Charles, had certainly been open enough with me. I liked him. He had a way about him that was appealing. He was probably not the best of sons, judging from his lack of communication with his mother, but who was I to pass judgment about something like that?

I went to the rack of keyboard instruments from which tiny red lights shone. I touched a key and an eerie, wailing, earsplitting scream came back at me from large speakers. Whatever happened to a good old acoustic piano? I wondered as I took a closer look at the other instruments. I picked up a mallet off the marimba and ran it across a set of wooden chimes that hung from the other rack. The sound was Oriental, or Middle Eastern, and pleasant. I did it again but wondered if I might be disturbing others in the building. I put the mallet down and smiled. If Joe Charles hadn't been disturbing others in the building when I arrived, no one ever would.

I perused the rest of the room. As I was looking at a photograph over the mattress of him performing with a musical group, the door to the bathroom slowly opened. Every muscle in my body tensed, and I braced. Then, I looked down and saw a large, fat, black-and-white cat come through the now open door and rub against the edge of it.

I breathed a sigh of relief and said the sort of silly things we always say to cats. True to its nature, the cat looked at me, then walked away with its back arched, stepped up onto the mattress, stretched, and curled into a ball.

I peeked in the bathroom. One of those portable plastic shower enclosures was in a corner. A chipped white-enamel sink was stained with rust. Beneath the sink was a low cardboard box that functioned as a litter box. Strips of newspaper lined its bottom. I leaned forward to better see the ripped-up news-print. Looking back at me was an eye; my eye. One of the strips had been torn in such a way that my eye from the front page of the *Post* was visible. Other strips from that same page were in the box, too.

I straightened and returned to the main room. Strange, I thought. Charles had said he knew Waldo was dead, but had not read about me. He said he didn't read newspapers, yet here was the edition of the *Post* on which my face was plastered all over Page One. Why would he lie about something like that?

The phone rang, a muffled sound; the instrument must have been smothered beneath something. I looked at the mattress and saw a black cord leading under pillows. The ringing stopped, and Joe Charles's voice said, 'I split

74

this scene for a while, but I'll make it back soon. Lay your message on me when you hear the A-flat, and I'll return the favor when I get back. *Ciao!*'

Then, the caller's voice was heard: 'Eleven tonight,' a man said. 'Usual place. Don't be late.' There was the sound of the phone being hung up, a series of beeps, and the room was silent again.

I cocked my head and narrowed my eyes as though that would help me think, the way I have to turn off the radio in a car when looking for a house number. Always someone else's car, of course. I don't drive.

I'd recognized the voice of the caller. Detective Alphonse Rizzi. I wasn't certain it was him, at least not enough to testify under oath, but it certainly sounded like him. Why would *he* be calling Joe Charles?

I contemplated replaying the message but the sound of footsteps on the metal stairs sent me back to the black chair. Charles came through the door carrying a brown paper bag. He took off his coat, opened the bag on the plastic box on which he'd been sitting and, on his knees, looked up at me. 'Sure you don't want something to eat?' he asked. He'd bought, along with his coffee and my tea, two packages of chocolate cake filled with a gooey white substance, undoubtedly terminally sweet.

'No, thank you. Just the tea will be fine.'

He handed me my cup, opened one of the

packages, and eagerly ate its goopy contents. He finished it in seconds and opened the second. I'd bought him a meal, maybe the only one he would have that day. He didn't mention change from my five dollars; I didn't ask.

'That's a pretty cat,' I said.

'Yeah, only he's getting fat. His name is Thelonious.'

'Interesting name.'

'I named him after Thelonious Monk.'

'The jazz musician,' I said, glad to demonstrate a little knowledge of his world. 'Did he play all these instruments?'

Charles laughed. 'Nah. This kind of electronic stuff wasn't around when he was working. He probably wouldn't have liked it anyway.' He looked at his watch. 'Look, Mrs Fletcher, I was in the middle of a composition that I have to have ready for tomorrow night. I'm afraid I have to cut this off.'

'Of course, I didn't mean to take from your composing time. Let me ask you this before I go. How did you and Waldo end up getting back together in New York?'

'He looked me up when he came from Colorado.'

'Why did he come to New York? If he was in the witness protection program, it would seem safer in Colorado.'

'Mrs Fletcher, I really have to get back to work.'

I stood. 'Waldo was accused of drug
76

smuggling in Maine. Was he involved in drugs here in New York?'

'Not that I know of.'

'The police say Waldo was murdered by drug dealers.'

'I wouldn't know about that.'

'Did he live here with you?' I asked.

'No.'

'Where did he live?'

'I really don't know. Somewhere around.'

'I promise I'll leave in a minute, but I have so many questions. What name did you call him?'

'Huh?'

'Waldo Morse, or Waldo Marsh?'

'How do you know . . . ?'

'That he used the name Marsh? It was on his ID the day he died. That was his name under the witness protection program.'

'Right.' Charles pulled my chair over to the keyboard rack, sat in it, and played a chord that reverberated throughout the room.

I went to the door. 'I would love to hear you perform, Joe. Where will you be tonight?'

'I don't have a gig tonight.'

'I'm afraid I don't know very much about jazz, but I thought I might learn a little while visiting New York. Can you recommend a good jazz club? I'm having dinner with business associates, but I'll be free by eleven and . . .'

He said quickly without looking at me, 'All over the city. Lots of jazz clubs in the Village, some fancier joints uptown.'

'Well, I wish I could hear you play. You said you had to have your composition ready for tomorrow night. Could I hear you then?'

I knew I was pushing it; the scowl on his round face confirmed it. 'You wouldn't enjoy my music, Mrs Fletcher. The kind of music I'm into is for young people. I figure you're more comfortable with Tommy Dorsey and Benny Goodman.'

I smiled. 'I loved those bands, but I'm not so old that I can't appreciate new things.'

'Thanks for the coffee and pastry.'

I wouldn't have called it pastry, but I suppose the word would do. I said as an afterthought, 'Do you have a phone? I would like to be able to call you.'

'It's out of order.'

'How do you get calls from people who want you to perform?' I asked.

'I use a service. Sorry, Mrs Fletcher, but I really have to get back to this.'

'Yes, and I apologize for not taking my cue earlier. You've been very kind.'

I was on my way down the metal stairs and had rounded the corner at the second level when a young woman raced up from the foyer and almost bumped into me. She mumbled an apology and kept going. I stepped back against the wall so that I could see the third floor and saw her run directly to Joe Charles's door, open it, and disappear inside. Charles had started playing his keyboard instruments the minute I was out of his apartment, but the music stopped abruptly. I lingered as long as I thought I could; I was tempted to go up and press my ear against the door, but was afraid I couldn't navigate the metal stairs in silence.

I went back out to Crosby Street, now covered with a dense, white layer of snow. It was beautiful; all the hard, dirty concrete that had been there when I'd arrived was hidden. I was struck with a sudden touch of nostalgia. Was it snowing in Cabot Cove?

CHAPTER TEN

The *Publishers Weekly* interview ended a little before five, which gave me an hour until my appointment with the *Village Voice* at Buckley House. Ruth Lazzara, who wasn't happy that I'd been unreachable, but didn't make too much of it, suggested a drink or a cup of coffee, but I told her I had errands to run.

I needed a walk to clear my head. The snow had tapered off, and the city was aglow with the lights reflecting off its crystalline ground cover. I walked slowly, enjoying store windows that were showcases for their owners' holiday wares. I stopped to admire a collection of cut glass. As I did, a shop I'd passed a few doors away came to mind. I'd considered going in but talked myself out of it. Silly, I'd told myself.

Too cloak-and-dagger. You're a grown woman, Jessica. Forget it.

I retraced my steps and stood in front of the other window once again. A few deep breaths and I was inside where a chubby young woman wearing clothes too tight for her figure, and chewing gum with enthusiasm, asked without enthusiasm if I needed help.

'Yes, I think so. I'm not quite sure the style I want. Perhaps if you show me a few models, I'll be able to decide.'

She didn't seem happy about having to get up from a stool behind the counter, but did and went to a wall on which the shop's merchandise was displayed. 'We have all these in stock,' she said.

'Quite a selection,' I said. 'I think what I'm after is something contemporary, modern. "With it," I suppose is the phrase. Could I see that one?'

She removed a coal black wig from a plastic, featureless head, and handed it to me. Her pained expression testified to what she was thinking. I ignored her, took the wig to a mirror, and put it over my short, *piccolopasso* red hair. It was a full wig that reached my shoulders and made my head appear twice as big, my face half its normal size. I cocked my head left and right, smiled at my image in the mirror, and turned to her. 'Yes, I think this is perfect. What do you think?'

'It's the last one I figured you'd pick,' she

said. 'It's not you.'

'Exactly,' I said. 'Yes, I'll take this one.' I removed the wig and handed it to her.

As she put my purchase into a small shopping bag and started to write out a sales receipt, I went to a revolving display stand of large, garish sunglasses, pulled a pair from the rack, checked myself in a mirror attached to the stand, and handed them to her. 'Please add these to the bill.' She looked at me with that same pained, quizzical expression. As I left the shop, she quickly placed a 'CLOSED' sign in the door. I could imagine her conversation that night with friends about the kooky woman who was her last customer.

Originally, the interview with the *Village Voice* was to be on the subject of the mystery genre and my views of it as an emerging force in mainstream publishing. But because of the hullabaloo about the Waldo Morse murder, the literary critic for the *Voice* was accompanied by an investigative reporter whose specialty was the Manhattan police beat. I parried their questions best I could, falling back time and again on the impropriety of discussing an ongoing murder investigation.

When I'd arrived at Buckley House, three members of the press were in the reception area. They'd been there all day, according to the receptionist, and must have been half-asleep. By the time they realized who I was, I was on my way through a door to the conference room. They were more alert when Ruth Lazzara and I came out of the interview. I fended off their questions as politely as possible, knowing that Ruth preferred that I sit with them.

She asked about my plans for the evening.

'A hot bath, a drink, a light dinner, and early to bed with a good murder mystery,' I said.

'See you in the morning, then, Jessica.'

'Yes, I have tomorrow's itinerary. Have a nice evening.'

Vaughan and Olga were at the apartment when I arrived. I changed into comfortable clothing, and we enjoyed a drink in the living room, Sadie and Rose flanking my chair. 'I've made a decision,' I said. 'I'm moving to a hotel tonight.'

They expressed their usual reasons why they didn't want me to do that, but I persisted. I'd stopped at a phone booth during the day and made a reservation at the Sheraton-Park Avenue, a small, European-style jewel at Park and Thirty-seventh Street that was my favorite whenever I visited New York. Eventually, the Buckleys accepted my decision. Vaughan said he would drive me.

As I packed, the phone rang several times, each a call from a reporter. Bobby Johnson of the *Post* called twice; Vaughan said Johnson had left several messages on the machine during the day.

'See?' I said. 'At least the phone might stop

ringing, and you can have some peace. All I ask is that you tell no one where I'm staying.'

'Of course,' Olga said.

'I'll have to inform certain people at the office,' Vaughan said.

'I realize that, but please keep the list to a minimum and ask them to be discreet. I'd like to consider myself purely altruistic in leaving you, but I think being in a neutral space will be good for me, too. You do understand?'

'Yes,' Vaughan said. 'Just as long as you promise you'll be at our Christmas Eve party.'

'I wouldn't miss it.' It was Wednesday, December eighteenth. Christmas was a week away.

'Well,' Vaughan said with a sigh, 'if you're set on going to the hotel, let's do it.'

We left the Dakota by a back entrance and went to a garage where Vaughan housed his Lincoln Town Car. A short time later I checked into the hotel. I explained my need for privacy to a clerk at the desk, who assured me that all calls would be screened, messages taken, and that no calls would be put through with the exception of the people I'd listed—Vaughan and Olga, and Ruth Lazzara.

Instead of a single room, I was given a small suite. It was lovely, decorated in antique reproductions chosen to complement the muted hues of the walls and thick carpeting. I unpacked my bags, carefully hung clothing in the closet, took a Manhattan Yellow Pages directory from the nightstand, and found the listings under 'LIMOUSINES'. I chose the one with the largest display ad and asked to be picked up at ten.

After an invigorating hot shower, I went to the hotel dining room where, at a partially obscured table, I satisfied my hunger with a cold lobster salad preceded by hot consumme, and indulged myself in a glass of white wine. I felt two things: First, I was more relaxed then I had been since arriving in New York. And, second, I would go through with my plan for the evening.

I returned to my suite and changed from the cosmopolitan, conservative clothing I'd worn to dinner into a pair of black slacks and black turtleneck sweater. I carefully adjusted the wig in front of the bathroom mirror, applied makeup heavier than usual, and put on the oversize sunglasses that had tiny silver chips in the upper corners. I leaned closer to the mirror: 'Is that you, Jessica?' I asked. I shook my head. If I couldn't tell it was me, no one else would.

Roy, my driver, was a handsome young black man in a black uniform, white shirt, black tie, and black peaked cap. Had he looked at me strangely when opening the door? Of course he had. I looked like a fool, at least in the genteel lobby of the Sheraton-Park Avenue. Hopefully, I would just be one of the crowd where I was going.

We headed for Crosby Street, near the corner of Bleecker, which was as much of a surprise to Roy as my appearance had been. But he was too much the courteous professional to overtly indicate his reaction, and drove slowly and skillfully down Park Avenue, sitting ramrod straight as the derelicts of the Bowery tried to solicit money from us. We finally pulled up to the curb at the designated spot. Roy waited a few moments before turning and asking, 'Ma'am?'

I leaned forward. 'I'd just like to sit here awhile if you don't mind.'

'Whatever you say.'

'I'm waiting for someone to come out of that doorway.' I pointed to the entrance to Joe Charles's building. 'If he does, I would like to follow him, but I don't want him to know it.'

'Yes, ma'am.'

'I suppose this represents an unusual assignment,' I said. 'I assure you we aren't breaking the law.'

His laugh was low and warm. 'Never entered my mind,' he said.

As I sat in the backseat and waited for Joe Charles to exit the building, I had trouble concentrating. How difficult it must be for law enforcement officers to conduct a stakeout hours on end. It's brain-numbing, to say nothing of the numbness that invaded other parts of my anatomy. I played all sorts of mind games to stay alert and to make sure no one came through that door without my knowing it.

My patience paid off. At twenty minutes to eleven, Joe Charles came through the door. He was accompanied by the young woman I'd seen going into his apartment. They got into a battered tan Honda Civic parked in front of the building. They had trouble starting the car. I hadn't wanted to alert them that we were there, so I waited until they'd finally managed to get the Honda up and running and had pulled away. 'That's the car I want to follow,' I told Roy. We fell into a comfortable distance behind them.

'I've never done this before,' Roy said over his shoulder. 'I mean, never followed a car.'

'You're doing just fine,' I said.

We eventually ended up on a very busy street in what looked to me to be Greenwich Village. Roy confirmed that's where we were. We hadn't traveled far. We were on Seventh Avenue South, between Bleecker and Grove streets.

The tan Honda pulled up to a vacant parking meter in front of a restaurant whose sign read 'SWEET BASIL'. 'What an interesting name,' I said.

'A good jazz club,' Roy said. 'They book only top musicians.'

I watched Charles and his female friend get out of the car and stand together on the sidewalk as though unsure of their next move. He had a manila envelope beneath his arm.

86

We'd parked at a hydrant at the end of the block, far enough so to not be seen by them, but close enough to observe their actions. They seemed to be arguing; I wished I had one of those exotic microphones to point at them and hear their words. Finally, after much debate, they entered Sweet Basil.

I had a real decision to make now. It was easy following them from the backseat of a chauffeured car. But that wasn't good enough. If I left it at that, it would have been a wasted exercise, to say nothing of expensive. I had to enter the club. Would my costume, wig, and uncharacteristic makeup keep them from recognizing me? I had a feeling it would. I said to Roy, 'I'm going inside. I probably won't be more than a hour. Will you wait for me?'

'Of course,' he said. 'If the police make me move, I'll be in the vicinity. Look for me.'

'I certainly will,' I said, touching his shoulder. 'Thank you for being so indulgent.'

'Indulgence is what I'm paid for,' he said. 'Enjoy the music.'

'I hadn't even thought about music,' I said, laughing. 'I'll finally get to hear some New York jazz.'

The music, loud and vibrating, hit me in the face as I opened the door. There were horns and drums, and the musicians playing them attacked their mission with zeal. A sign outside said the group was known as the Harper Brothers. I'd never heard of them, but I was certainly hearing them now.

One of my suppositions was correct. I did not seem out of place in my garb and wig. No one looked askance at me. An attractive young man asked if I wished a table in the music room. I said I preferred to sit at the bar, and he led me to a vacant stool at the far end of it, which gave me a perfect view of the music room that was at the rear of the club. The only problem was I couldn't see very much through my dark glasses. I lowered them. Joe Charles and his female companion had taken a table in the barroom, next to the music room entrance. I'd been right about the voice on Charles's answering machine. Seated at their table was Detective Alphonse Rizzi.

I tried to analyze the overall mood at the table. It wasn't anger, but it wasn't a backslapping get-together either. Rizzi did most of the talking, and Joe Charles listened intently, seeming to agree with what the detective was saying. The girl's dour, angry expression indicated something else.

It had become unbearably hot. Sweet Basil's heating system would have handled the entire State of Maine outdoors. I sipped from the Pink Lady I'd ordered, and dabbed at perspiration on my forehead and nose with a bar napkin. What made the heat even worse was the wig. It was like being under a hair dryer, and I had this driving obsession to rip it off my head. The collar of my black turtleneck seemed to have shrunk three sizes. All in all, I was uncomfortable, and considered getting up and leaving. There was nothing more to be gained by staying because I couldn't hear what they were saying. But my mission had been accomplished; Joe Charles and Detective Rizzi knew each other, and obviously had some sort of business between them.

Rizzi waved the waitress over and handed her money. Good. They were leaving, which meant I could, too.

'Hey baby, what's happening?'

The questioner was a gaunt, older man on my left wearing glasses even darker than mine. His smile revealed a dentist's pension. 'Pardon?' I said.

'What's happenin', baby,' he repeated. 'I haven't seen you here before. You dig the scene?'

'Dig this scene? Do I like it? Oh, yes, very much. Do you?'

'It wigs me, baby.'

'Wigs you?' For a moment, I thought he was referring to my wig. Then I realized it must be a jazz lover's expression that meant he liked it.

'Yeah, it's bad. Real bad.'

I fought my confusion and looked to where Charles, Rizzi, and the girl were making their way toward the door. I quickly put money on the bar and stood. Now, from a higher vantage point, I could see beneath the vacant table. The envelope Joe Charles had carried into the club was on the floor next to his chair. Did I dare scoop it up, examine its contents, maybe learn something more about him that might relate to his relationship with Rizzi, perhaps even to Waldo Morse's murder?

'Excuse me,' I said to the gentleman to my left.

'Bags is at the Blue Note,' he said, grasping my wrist. 'What say we make it over there?'

I removed his hand from my wrist, headed for the empty table, and sat in one of the chairs. I took off my sunglasses and wig, shoved them into my purse, reached down and picked up the envelope. It was sealed with tape. Open it there or take it with me? I decided on the latter and was about to head for the natural air conditioning outside when Joe Charles burst through the door and came directly to the table. He looked at me, his eyes wide, his expression angry. I didn't know what else to do, so I smiled. He snatched the envelope from my hands.

'Hello,' I said.

He seemed to want to say something, but words didn't come. He pressed his lips together, his eyes turned hard and he left, almost knocking over other tables on his way.

'Nicely done, Jessica,' I said aloud. 'Smooth. Real smooth.'

CHAPTER ELEVEN

After a jittery night's sleep at the hotel—one recurring dream had me naked, except for my wig and sunglasses, standing in front of a large audience that laughed long and loud—I awoke with a start at six. 'How could you have been so stupid?' were my first words as I went to the window and drew open the drapes. It was dark, not because dawn hadn't broken, but because the sky was heavy and low. It looked like snow; if I were outside, I knew I would smell it.

I called the hotel operator for messages.

'I have seven for you, Mrs Fletcher, and there are a lot of reporters in the lobby. They all keep asking me to call your room, but I told them I wouldn't.'

'Thank you. I appreciate that.' She gave me the seven messages, two of which were from Seth Hazlitt in Cabot Cove, and two from *Post* reporter Bobby Johnson. How did they know I'd moved to a hotel? How did anybody know aside from the Buckleys, and Ruth Lazzara? I thought the Cabot Cove gossip mill was a threat to personal privacy, but I'd never seen anything like this. People say that the best place to lose yourself is in a large city. You couldn't get me to testify to it.

I showered and dressed, then ordered half a

grapefruit, an English muffin, and a pot of tea from room service. While I waited for it to be delivered, I called Seth. 'Seth, it's Jessica. How in the world did you know I was here at this hotel?'

'I called the Buckleys. They said you were out, but after I said it was important that I talk to you, they told me where you were. I guess they know you and I are pretty good friends.'

'I talk about you often. What's so important?'

'Gettin' you to come home. I keep hearin' news reports about Waldo's murder and how you witnessed it. 'Course, they don't say his name, keep sayin' the Santa Claus was an unidentified drifter sort 'a fella, but I know. They say he was killed by a bunch of drug runners, and you know what they're like, Jess. They don't care that you're a nice woman and a famous writer. I want you to pack up your bags and get home here.' Before I could respond, he added, 'It's one thing for Jessica Fletcher not to be here for New Year's Eve, but it don't seem right you won't be here for Christmas, either.'

The timing of Seth's request was perfect. One of the things I'd contemplated while showering was going to Cabot Cove to see whether Nancy Morse knew about her husband's death. If not, I'd break the news.

There was more than altruism behind my decision, however. Nancy might be able to fill some holes, answer questions I'd been formulating since witnessing the murder. I wanted a chance to speak with her face-to-face. Informing her of Waldo's death would be as good an excuse as any.

'I am coming home sooner than planned,' I told Seth.

'Good to hear you talkin' sense again, Jessica.' He'd adopted a fatherly tone, as he often did when dismayed at something I was doing, or not doing. I loved him for it, but it could also be annoying.

'I won't be there for Christmas, Seth, but I am coming home tomorrow. Here's what I'd like you to do. I'll grab the first shuttle in the morning and fly to Boston. Would you be good enough to have Jed Richardson pick me up at Logan Airport and fly me home?' Jed Richardson owned Jed's Flying Service in Cabot Cove. I hate small planes. Come to think about it, I don't like big ones much, either. But I trusted Jed. And because I was trying to compress time, having him pick me up in Boston would save many hours.

'Ayuh,' Seth said. 'I'll call Jed as soon as I get off the phone. You say you'll take the first shuttle tomorrow morning. That'd be Friday. What time does the first shuttle arrive?'

'Friday? No, I'm coming on Saturday.'

'But you said tomorrow. Today's Thursday. Tomorrow's Friday.'

'God, I'm losing days already. Make it

93

Saturday morning. I'll check what time the first shuttle leaves and get back to you.'

'You are stubborn, Jessica.'

'I know.'

He sighed. 'How long will you be stayin'?'

'It won't be long. Be a dear and be at Jed's hangar when we arrive.'

'You don't have to ask. I already made a note to pick you up. Now, about how long you're stayin'. My advice is to pack all your belongin's and have them with you when you honk on up here on Saturday. Heah?'

'Yes, I hear you, Seth.'

I was happy to get off the phone. Seth had a tenacious side that dictated not letting go when he was adamant about something, especially when it concerned me. On the other hand, as I dwelled on his advice, the thought of leaving New York and being in Cabot Cove for the holidays was fiercely appealing.

I didn't have a lot of time to think about it, however. I was due to be picked up by Ruth Lazzara within the hour for a television talk show. I ate breakfast and read the *New York Times* that came with it. Unlike the *Post*, the *Times* had covered Waldo's murder as a small item deep inside. I didn't see any mention of it this morning, for which I was grateful.

The first face I saw as I stepped out of the elevator into the lobby was Bobby Johnson.

'Good morning, Mrs Fletcher.' He immediately grabbed my arm and propelled me

94

away from the other reporters, said in urgent, whispered tones, 'We have to talk.'

'I think that's the last thing we have to do, Mr Johnson.'

'Yeah?' He carried that morning's edition of the *Daily News* folded under his arm. He snapped it open and held it in front of my face. There, on Page One, blown up to gigantic proportions, was a picture of Waldo Morse in his Santa Claus costume at the moment he was shot. I stared at the picture. 'Where did they get this?' I asked.

'That's one of the pictures you took, isn't it?' he said.

'I don't know. It looks like . . .'

'It has to be. I told you I could make a great deal for you with those pictures. I really feel betrayed, Mrs Fletcher. I mean, I was the one who originally broke the story. I figured you owed me something.'

'Owed you?' I was poised to argue the point but a more important question came to mind. It had to be one of the photographs I'd taken, which meant the person who removed the roll of film from my purse had given it, or sold it, to the *News*. Who would have done such a thing?

Now, other reporters pressed close, and Ruth tried to appease them. 'I'm sure Mrs Fletcher will be happy to talk to all of you at some point,' she said, 'but she's due for a television show and we're running late.' Johnson took one of my arms, Ruth the other, and they virtually lifted me off the ground and headed for the exit to Park Avenue and a waiting limousine. Johnson started to get in the back with us, but I said in a voice that came as close to a growl as I could muster, 'Leave this minute, Mr Johnson. I don't know who gave that photograph to the *Daily News*, but I intend to find out who stole it from me. Leave me alone!'

He hesitated; would my bite be as strong as my bark? He slowly backed out, saying, 'Please, give me ten minutes sometime today.'

'Maybe,' I said. 'Maybe.'

He slammed the door, leaving Ruth and me alone in the backseat that was separated from the driver by a Plexiglas partition. Buckley House's publicist said, 'Mrs Fletcher, this is getting out of hand. I know that all this media attention creates a lot of tension for you. At the same time, we have a golden opportunity to milk every avenue of publicity for your new book. That benefits not only Buckley House, but you, too, in a very tangible way. I would like to schedule a press conference.'

'A press conference?' My laugh was involuntary. 'Press conferences are to announce budget cuts at the Pentagon, invasions, declarations of war.'

'Believe me, Mrs Fletcher, this story ranks right along with those. Please. Let me schedule one.'

'When?'

'I want to have enough time to properly notify everyone. How about Saturday? Saturday is a slow news day. We might get major space out of it.'

'Sorry, but I won't be available this weekend.'

'What do you mean you won't be available?' The words exploded from her lips.

'I need a day off, maybe two. I decided to hibernate this weekend, collect my thoughts, get a decent night's sleep. I need that.'

Her voice softened. 'Yes, I understand. I know I've been pushing pretty hard. How about Sunday afternoon? That would give you all of Saturday and Sunday morning to rest up. Could I schedule it for Sunday afternoon?'

'I'd prefer Monday, if we have to do it at all.'

'Sunday is better, believe me. Come Monday and the papers and stations get too busy. Sunday is perfect. If we give them enough provocative material on Sunday, they'll give us plenty of space and time on Monday.'

The thought of facing a press conference was overwhelming. But I knew I couldn't continue to disappoint her, or Vaughan Buckley. No matter how distasteful I found the experience, I did have a certain obligation, and I like to think of myself as a person who meets her obligations. Sunday afternoon would work. I would be in Cabot Cove Saturday and Saturday night, and fly back Sunday morning. One thing I was determined not to do, however, was to

97

tell Lazzara or anyone else that I was leaving the city.

I agreed to the press conference.

The TV interview went smoothly, although it took concentration on my part to focus upon what was being asked. That had become a pattern since witnessing Waldo Morse's murder—physically being in one place, my mind in another. As I sat beneath the glaring, hot lights of the television studio and discussed my working habits, my thoughts were really on Detective Alphonse Rizzi and Joe Charles. It was like waiting for the proverbial other shoe to drop. The first had hit the floor with a resounding thud when Joe Charles came back into Sweet Basil and saw me sitting at the table, sans wig and glasses. The second shoe, of course, was what they would do now that I'd confirmed a relationship between them. I'd reasoned during my restless night in the hotel that much depended upon the motive for their clandestine meeting in a jazz club at eleven o'clock at night. If it was for a good reason—a rational, legal, moral reason—it shouldn't bother them that I'd snuck in and observed. On the other hand, if there was something nefarious about their rendezvous, I might have more to worry about. The worst thing was not knowing which of the two scenarios was the true one. I was tempted to call Rizzi and confront him openly, but the morning was too rushed for that. Still, it was an option to consider, just as returning to Joe Charles's apartment to confront him was another.

'Pardon?'

'Oh, sorry, my mind wandered for a moment. I don't know how anyone can concentrate under all these lights and with all these wires underfoot,' I said.

'You get used to it, Mrs Fletcher. I was asking whether you always know the ending of your books before you start writing them.'

I answered that question, and others. Eventually, it was over and we left, Ruth praising me too much, I thought, for my performance. Fortunately, it had been taped. The daydreaming segments could be cut away.

'What's next?' I asked.

'An interview with *Voice of America*,' she said. 'It's on your itinerary.'

'I'm looking forward to that one,' I said. 'I've never been interviewed by a government agency before.'

'The interviewer, Dave Hubler, will be in Washington,' she told me. 'You'll be sitting in the New York studio and hear his questions over earphones. When it's done, he'll take your answers and weave them into a finished show. He's terrific at it. It will be translated into many languages.'

'Now I'm even more excited,' I said. 'Are you still planning a press conference for Sunday afternoon.'

'Absolutely, which is why I have to get back

to the office the minute we leave VOA. Sorry I can't have lunch with you. You do know about the *People* interview at three?'

'Yes. I'll be on time. I'm so far behind in my Christmas shopping. I'll try to squeeze some in before that interview.'

A million other people were evidently behind in their shopping, too, judging from the crowded stores. I stopped at Barnes & Noble on lower Fifth Avenue and stocked up on all the books on my list (mostly books for me; I bought a few as gifts and had them shipped home to avoid having to haul extra weight with me). My next stop was Caswell-Massey on Lexington where I bought pretty fragrances for female friends, including almond cream and cucumber soaps. I was running out of time. One more shop—F.A.O. Schwarz, and a collection of toys for the little ones on my list. If I didn't have that three-o'clock interview with *People*, I would have stayed the afternoon in the fabled toy store's fantasyland.

The reporter from *People* asked few questions about my work but many about my personal life, including romantic interests, which conjured up pleasant, unstated thoughts of George Sutherland in London. A photographer from the magazine took dozens of shots under the theory, I assumed, that if you take enough, you're bound to come up with a usable one. They also announced they wanted to photograph me at home in Cabot Cove when

I returned. I agreed.

'Dinner plans?' Ruth asked as we sat alone in the conference room that had been the scene of the interview.

'No, and delighted I don't. I can't wait for a quiet evening in that lovely suite.'

There were myriad messages for me at the hotel, including one from Vaughan Buckley marked 'URGENT.' I was immediately put through to him at Buckley House. 'Jessica, glad you got back to me. I just missed you and Ruth at *People*. I received word this afternoon that the *Times* review of your book is a rave.'

'How thoughtful of you to call with that news.'

'It gets even better. The *Times* wants to do a profile on you for the same issue the review will appear in, a week from Sunday. I set up dinner this evening with the writer doing the piece.'

'Tonight? I was looking forward to doing nothing.'

'I imagine you were,' he said, laughing, 'considering the schedule you've been on. But Jess, this is a golden opportunity. By having an interview appear in tandem with a great review, it takes you and the book to another plateau. This was a last-minute decision on the *Times'* part. We can't disappoint them.'

I sighed deeply. I knew he was right. I would go along with the interview because it was expected of me. At the same time, I had a nagging and painful desire to be transported magically from the suite and from Manhattan to my comfortable, familiar living room in Cabot Cove, a fire crackling in the large fireplace, and me dressed in my best no-visitors outfit.

'All right,' I said. 'Where and when?'

'Le Cirque. I'll have a car pick you up at the hotel at eight.'

'I'll be ready.'

With another dinner staring me in the face, true and total relaxation was out of the question. I paced the suite, becoming increasingly angry at my inability to turn off the world and to wind down. I took a fast shower, changed into what I would wear that evening, and went downstairs. I'd become paranoid enough to expect members of the press to be hovering outside the elevator door whenever I walked through it. But that wasn't the case tonight. I walked on Park Avenue to Fortieth Street and found a cab. 'Crosby Street, at Bleecker.'

Once again, I stood alone on the street in front of the converted warehouse in which Joe Charles lived. I watched the taxi disappear around a corner, its red tail lights trailing away like a rescue ship that had missed me. It was bitter cold. I pulled the collar of my crimson cloth coat tight around my neck and the back of my head, and took deep breaths to stave off my shivering. I wasn't sure where the cold left off and fear began. It really didn't matter. I had acted on impulse, as though some force over which I had no control had dictated I be there, that I confront Joe Charles before he, or Detective Rizzi, took the initiative.

I crossed the street and looked up at the building. There were a few lights on in apartments on upper floors, but not many. The entrance door was still ajar. I pushed it open and stepped into the depressing, odorous lobby. The inner door was open, too. I placed one foot on the first step of the metal staircase and listened, hoping to hear music from Charles's floor. There was only a stagnant, unnatural silence. No people talking, laughing, arguing, and certainly no music.

I ascended the staircase slowly to keep my footsteps from ringing out, and paused at his door. I poised to knock. If no one was home, knocking on the door was academic—and safe. Another deep breath, and a rap of my knuckles.

What was the sound that came from inside? A gasp? A startled cry? I placed my ear against the door and focused on the sound. It had stopped. Quiet now. Should I knock again? No need. I placed my hand on the doorknob, slowly turned it, and pushed it open. A dim shaft of light from a street lamp outside splashed a faint yellow ribbon across the floor. I surveyed the room. I could see the end of it where the array of musical instruments had been. They were gone. Was Charles out on a playing job, a 'gig' as he would call it?

In order to see the other half of the room, I had to enter. I was reluctant because of the noise I'd heard when I knocked, but what was to be gained by having again come here and not following through? Chances were he'd gone out to play his instruments in some nightclub, that the apartment was empty, and that—

I saw the source of the sound I'd heard. The cat crossed the room and sat in a corner, like one of those feline doorstops sold at art fairs. I had nothing to fear by going inside. Was it a breach of etiquette to do that? Of course it was, just as having contemplated stealing the envelope in Sweet Basil wasn't especially ladylike, to say nothing of legal. But I wasn't there to steal anything.

'Hello,' I said softly.

I heard the noise again. I looked at the cat. He was still curled up in the corner.

'Hello,' I repeated. 'This is Jessica Fletcher. Joe? Are you here?'

Hearing nothing, I took bold steps through the door and looked to my left; a light was on in the bathroom.

I again scrutinized the main room. It was empty, no musical instruments, no bed, no chairs, nothing except cardboard boxes piled in front of the window. Charles must have moved. Because I'd bumbled upon him and Rizzi in Sweet Basil? Maybe, although there could be other reasons—maybe a sudden playing job opportunity in another city. No, that was silly. He'd bolted. Because of me.

I turned and squarely faced the closed bathroom. The light seeping under the door seemed to have intensified in brightness, as though a rheostat had been turned up.

I considered leaving, running down the stairs and finding the first transportation uptown. That would have been the sensible thing to do. But as Seth Hazlitt often accused me, I was not always the most sensible of people. Prudent in many aspects of my life, certainly reasonable in selected areas, but not always sensible, at least according to his definition.

I approached the bathroom door and, after a long, deep breath to fill myself with courage, opened it.

She came directly at me. It happened fast; all was a blur. I instinctively fell out of the way, my back smashing against the wall. Her forward momentum carried her slightly past me, a toilet plunger held high in both hands.

'I'm not here to hurt you. I'm Jessica Fletcher. I was a friend of . . .'

My words froze her. She slowly lowered the plunger and faced me. It was the girl I'd seen entering the apartment the first time I was there, and who was with Charles at Sweet Basil. She was a pretty little thing, although the fright on her face masked much of her beauty. She wore jeans and a red-and-black flannel shirt. I forced a smile and said gently, 'You can put that down. I just came here hoping to see Joe again. It looks as though I'm late.' I gestured to the empty room. 'He's gone?'

She lowered the plunger and stared at me, helpless, confused, every muscle in her slender body coiled. Then, as though she were an ice statue that had been hit by a sudden blast of hot air, she visibly relaxed. The plunger fell to the floor. She looked down at it, kicked it across the room, and followed the path it took.

'I saw you with Joe at Sweet Basil.'

She said without turning, 'Yes, I know. He told me when he got in the car. He was furious.'

'He had every right to be. Was Detective Rizzi angry, too?'

She laughed, her back still to me. 'Mad enough to kill,' she said.

'I didn't mean to upset anyone to that extent,' I said, walking to the boxes piled near the window and sitting on them. 'What is your name?' I asked.

She faced me. 'Susan Kale.'

I took in the empty room. 'Joe has left?'

She nodded.

'For good? Do you know where he's gone?'

'I have no idea.'

'Then what about these?' I asked, patting the boxes on either side of me. 'How will you know where to send them?'

'They're my things. I packed them.'

'You lived here with Joe?'

'Yes. And with Waldo sometimes.'

106

'With Waldo? I assumed you were Joe's girlfriend.'

She said ruefully, 'What difference does it make? Joe is gone, and Waldo is dead.'

'Yes, of course,' I said. 'I suppose you know I witnessed Waldo's murder.'

'You should have looked the other way.'

'That's what I've been thinking ever since it happened. I would like to know more about Waldo, especially his life here in New York. I thought Joe would be able to help me. Now that he's gone, would you fill me in about Waldo?'

She'd become calm, almost catatonic. Now she stiffened, her pretty, soft mouth stretched into a hard line. 'Why should I talk to you or anybody else?'

'You don't have to, of course. I have no official connection with Waldo's murder.'

'Then why . . . ?'

'Why am I here? Why did I go to such ridiculous lengths to follow you and Joe to Sweet Basil? Because, as my friends back in Maine say, I was born to snoop.' I laughed. 'Here I am snooping again, and this time it's on you. I want to be your friend, Susan. I wish you no harm, but I do need to sort this out. After all, I was a witness to a murder. That doesn't give me a legal right to ask questions, but it certainly makes my interest understandable. Don't you agree?'

'What good are answers going to be, Mrs

107

Fletcher? It won't bring them back.'

'You make it sound as though Joe is dead, too.'

'Maybe he is.'

'It looks to me as though he moved. To avoid being dead? Is that a possibility?'

'You bet it is,' she said.

It was the first sign of spark she'd exhibited, and I was happy to see it. 'Who would he be running from?'

'Everybody.'

'That's a big cast.'

'Look, Mrs Fletcher, this is all very nice but I have to get out of here, too. I need to find a place to live, a place to—'

'To hide?'

'Call it what you want.' A heavy navy pea jacket was on one of the boxes. She put it on.

'I have a suggestion.'

'What's that?'

'That you stay with me for a few days. I have a lovely suite in a very nice hotel. The couch in the living room opens up. You'd be safe and secure there. Besides—'

'Besides, you'd have me around to question.'

I smiled. 'Yes. My offer is not entirely altruistic. Will you?'

'I don't know. I don't know anything.'

'It would give you time to collect your thoughts. I promise you don't have to answer any questions if you don't want to.' Her eyes narrowed into skeptical slits. 'I promise. I keep my promises.'

'Maybe.'

'That's better than a flat refusal. Tell you what. I'm staying at the Sheraton-Park Avenue. It's at Thirty-seventh Street and Park. I have to go to a very important dinner. I'll leave instructions with the desk that when you arrive, you're to be given a key to the suite. Do you have some identification that will prove to them you're Susan Kale?'

She nodded.

'Good. I know I can't force you to do this, but I urge you to. Bring Thelonious.'

'I call her Miss Hiss.'

'Miss Hiss is certainly welcome. I should be back to the hotel by eleven, certainly no later than midnight. In fact, I'll make sure I am. I hope you'll be there.'

I rose from the boxes and extended my hand. She seemed unsure whether to touch me, but did. I took her slender hands in mine and squeezed. 'I think between the two of us, Susan, things might work out just fine.' I gave an extra squeeze for emphasis and left.

*   *   *

I stopped at the hotel, left instructions about Susan, and was ready when the limo arrived to take me to Le Cirque.

I'd expected to see Ruth Lazzara at dinner, but she wasn't there. It was just Vaughan

Buckley and the *Times* writer. Again I had to force myself to focus on the conversation because my mind kept snapping back to the hotel. Would Susan Kale show up?

After dinner, Vaughan drove me back to the Sheraton-Park Avenue. As we sat in front of the entrance, the car's heater staving off the outside freeze, he said, 'You have a lot on your mind, don't you?'

'Yes, I do.' I paused, said, 'You said you'd make this evening up to me, Vaughan.'

'You name it.'

'Give me tomorrow night off.'

'I don't think anything was scheduled for tomorrow night. You can check with Ruth in the morning.'

'Schedules don't seem to mean much these days. There's always something coming up at the last minute. I desperately need some time to myself.' I placed my hand on his sleeve and smiled. 'Don't misunderstand. I'm grateful for everything you've done for me and the book, but I'm afraid I'm one of those creatures— maybe just a typical writer—who needs think-time. Ruth has scheduled a press conference for Sunday afternoon, and I'll be there. There's a book signing tomorrow morning. I'll be at that, too. But after it, I'd love to hibernate, become a bear in the woods.'

'Then that's exactly what you'll do, Jessica. Go on, get to bed. And thanks for being there tonight.'

I opened the door to my suite and called Susan's name to an empty living room. She wasn't in the bedroom, either, or the bath.

'Damn!' I said. Foolish girl. I'd offered her sanctuary, and she'd shunned it.

It was quarter of twelve. The sensible decision would have been to simply go to bed and hope she showed up later that night, or the next day. But I knew I wouldn't sleep.

I called the car service I'd used before and asked to be picked up as quickly as possible. The car arrived fifteen minutes later. When I told the driver to take me to Crosby Street, he gave me the same strange look that Roy, my previous driver, had given me. We pulled up in front of the converted warehouse. 'Please wait for me,' I said.

'Here?' He looked out at the deserted, dark street.

'I won't be long.' He got out and opened my door.

As I crossed the street, I saw him get back into the car like a man possessed, and heard the snap of electronic door locks.

I bounded up the stairs without concern for any noise my shoes made on the metal, went directly to Joe Charles's door, and tried it. It opened. All the lights were off but there was sufficient light from outside to see Miss Hiss curled up next to what appeared to be a person in a sleeping bag.

'Susan,' I said.

The only response came from the cat. It stood, hunched its back, and curled up again against the form on the floor.

I stepped inside. 'Susan,' I said louder this time. Still nothing. I went to the sleeping bag and looked down. My eyes widened, a cry caught in my throat. It was no sleeping bag. It was a shower curtain wrapped around the body of Susan Kale.

I picked up the cat, left the apartment, went down the stairs, and crossed the street to where my driver jumped out to open the door. I scrambled inside and let the cat out of my arms. 'Take us to the nearest phone booth.'

'Is something wrong?' he asked.

'Something is very wrong. And this cat's name is Miss Hiss. She's going to need a home.'

CHAPTER TWELVE

'And that's all you know about the deceased?'

I stood in the middle of the apartment with two detectives, an assortment of uniformed police, a couple of lab technicians, and a police photographer. I'd called 911 from the first booth we came to, and the dispatcher directed me to return to the scene and wait. I followed her instructions to the extent that I went back to Crosby Street, but didn't go to the apartment. I stayed in the limo with the driver and Miss Hiss until the first patrol cars arrived, sirens blaring, roof lights tossing twisted, disorienting red pulses into the air.

The detectives were courteous and businesslike; I was disappointed Rizzi wasn't one of them.

I said to the officer who questioned me, 'Yes, that's all I know about her. She said her name was Susan Kale. She was the girlfriend of a young man who lived here. Joe Charles.'

The detective looked around the room, now flooded with lights powered by a portable generator. 'Doesn't look to me like *anybody* lived here.'

'Joe Charles has disappeared. I was here earlier today and spoke with Ms Kale. I asked her to stay with me at my hotel because I thought her life might be in danger.'

'What made you think that?'

'Because her boyfriend disappeared so suddenly. That struck me as unusual. Doesn't it strike you that way?'

He grunted. He obviously was more comfortable asking questions than answering them. I, of course, was again faced with the dilemma of how much to tell him, especially about my knowledge of Rizzi's familiarity with Joe Charles and the dead girl. They'd been together at Sweet Basil the night before. Should I mention that? I was hesitant to involve Rizzi, not out of any feelings for him but because I was afraid. Yes, afraid. To link

113

him with Susan Kale and Joe Charles, and to further identify any possible connection between them and Waldo Morse—also a murder victim—could create a major scandal, one in which I would be hopelessly mired.

There was, of course, the possibility—perhaps even the probability—that Rizzi knowing these people meant absolutely nothing. I had no knowledge of what they talked about at the jazz club. As far as I know, there is nothing in the rule book prohibiting a detective from enjoying an off-duty night out.

This detective, whose name was Santana, lowered his notebook to his side and slowly shook his head. 'You know, Mrs Fletcher, this is the second murder you've been involved with.'

'"Involved with?" I happened to be at the wrong place at the wrong time when Santa Claus was shot, and I discovered this body because I met a young girl and cared about her. I wouldn't call that "being involved."'

'Call it what you want, Mrs Fletcher, but you sure do have a lousy sense of time and place.'

I asked if I could leave.

'In a minute.' He issued orders to a technician, then went to a corner where he perched on a windowsill and wrote in his book. I gave him a few minutes before approaching. He looked up and raised his eyebrows.

'Detective Santana, is Detective Rizzi on-duty tonight?'

'Al? No, he comes on in the morning.'

'What time?'

Santana shrugged. 'Eight, eight-thirty.'

'Thank you very much.' I started to walk away.

'Mrs Fletcher.'

'Yes?'

'Leave Rizzi out of this.'

I closed the gap between us. 'Leave him out of this? Why would I do that? He was involved with my first poor sense of time and place, and I . . .'

We both turned as the apartment door opened. A uniformed patrolman stepped inside and said to Santana, 'The Fonz is here.'

'The Fonz?' I said.

'The . . . Forget it,' Santana said. He announced to others in the room, 'Shape up. The commissioner is here.'

The commissioner? The Fonz? They call the police commissioner of New York 'The Fonz'?

A tall, heavyset man wearing an expensive black overcoat, and with a head of thick salt-and-pepper hair entered.

Why would the police commissioner be interested in the murder of a girl on Crosby Street? I didn't have to wait long for the answer. With an engaging broad smile on his handsome, tanned face, he crossed the room and extended his hand. 'Mrs Fletcher.'

'Yes. You're Commissioner . . .' I had no idea what his name was.

'I'm Police Commissioner Frye, Ferdinand Frye. It's a real pleasure to meet you Mrs Fletcher. I've been a fan for years.'

Was he being honest, or trying to flatter me? He put that doubt to rest when he mentioned two of my older books, and referred to one of the characters by name.

'I really should offer an apology to you, Mrs Fletcher. Here you are in New York promoting your latest best-seller, and all you seem to come upon are murders. Hardly the way to welcome one of the world's most distinguished writers to our city.'

His charm—he dripped with it—took me off-guard. Whether he was an effective police commissioner remained conjecture, but he certainly made an engaging official greeter for the city of New York.

'I wonder if I might have a word with you in private, Mrs Fletcher?'

'Of course.'

He led me past technicians drawing diagrams on the floor to the small, shabby bathroom and closed the door behind us. 'Mrs Fletcher, I'm sure you have your share of crime in Cabot Cove, and I'm also sure that your law enforcement officers there are first-rate.'

'That's true,' I said.

Commissioner Frye's face twisted into a grimace. He shoved his hands deep into his overcoat pockets and said, 'The problem is, Mrs Fletcher, in a city like New York, crime sometimes gets complicated.' He scrutinized me through narrowed eyes. 'Do you know what I mean?'

'I don't think so. Are you talking about the murder of this young girl tonight?'

'Maybe. The point is there are forces at work that sometimes turn simple murders into complicated ones for me and my department.'

He waited for my response. I didn't know what to say, so I said, 'I still don't understand, but I'll accept your statement.'

'Good.' That big smile washed over his face again.

We looked at each other in silence. What was I supposed to say next?

He broke the quiet. 'Tell you what, Mrs Fletcher. The mayor has personally instructed me to extend to you every courtesy of the city. He's authorized me to pick up all your expenses while you're here, hotel, meals, the works.'

'That's very generous, Commissioner Frye, but all my expenses are paid by my publisher.'

'We thought they probably were, so we'd like to offer something above and beyond expenses. How would you like a free vacation—in the Bahamas?'

Free? Is there such a thing as a free vacation or lunch? I smiled. So did he. 'Why?' I asked. 'You say you've been authorized to offer me this. An offer is usually in return for a service. What service am I to give?'

'Ah, the mind of a mystery writer at work.' He laughed. 'Mrs Fletcher, there are no strings. As I said, we're unhappy that your trip to the city has ended up with witnessing one murder, and discovering the body of another victim. The mayor wants to make it up to you.'

'Well, that is very generous of the mayor, but I'm afraid it isn't necessary. No, I really don't need, or want, a vacation paid for by New York City.'

'Suit yourself, Mrs Fletcher. The mayor does feel strongly, however, that he does not want you to suffer any further unpleasant incidents while you're our guest. I'm assigning twenty-four-hour security for the duration of your stay.'

I suppose my face reflected my confusion. 'Do you think my life is in danger?' I asked.

That easy, pleasant laugh again. 'No, not at all. But we know how much pressure has been put upon you by the press. I'm afraid that pressure is going to become even more intense. There must be fifty media vultures waiting downstairs.'

'That's dreadful.'

'But understandable, considering your fame as a mystery writer and the publicity you generated by witnessing the murder of that sidewalk Santa. We'd feel better knowing that you're under our protection day and night. You know, New York City doesn't have the best reputation with the rest of the country. Johnny

Carson and other TV comics saw to that. We want to make sure that you—that *we* don't give them any more grist for negative humor.'

I shook my head. 'I do not want a policeman with me twenty-four hours a day.'

'Afraid you don't have much say about it, Mrs Fletcher. I have a responsibility for the safety of the citizens of this city, including visitors.'

I shrugged. 'I suppose there is nothing I can do about it. I probably should be grateful. I'm not.' I opened the door and looked into the living room where technicians were still at work. I said to Commissioner Frye, 'I'm suddenly very tired. I'd like to go back to my hotel.'

'Of course. I have a car waiting downstairs. I assume you gave a statement to the detectives.'

'Yes, as brief as it was. I really didn't know anything aside from having discovered her body, poor thing.'

I started to leave the bathroom but stopped in the doorway, turned, and said, 'Detective Rizzi. Will he be assigned to this murder?'

Frye frowned. 'Rizzi? No. He's narcotics. Why do you ask?'

'Just that he was the detective with whom I spoke after witnessing the murder of the Santa on Fifth Avenue. I felt comfortable with him, that's all. If I am to have constant contact with the police, I would appreciate having Detective Rizzi assigned to my detail.'

Frye grunted. 'I'll see what I can do,' he said without conviction.

The commissioner and two uniformed patrolmen escorted me down the steps and to the front door of the building. An hour ago, Crosby Street had been eerily deserted. Now, it was a jumble of police cars, ambulances, media vehicles, cops, reporters, and dozens of onlookers drawn to the scene like moths to a summer candle. The moment I appeared, harsh lights controlled by television crews came to life, along with strobes from still photographers.

'Let us through, let us through,' Frye said as he led me to a black, unmarked sedan. Two officers stiffened as we approached; one opened the back door. Frye said, 'These two officers are assigned to you tonight. They'll be relieved in the morning.'

'The quiet little hotel I'm staying at will not appreciate this,' I said.

'Can't be helped, Mrs Fletcher.'

I suddenly remembered my car and driver, and Miss Hiss. 'Excuse me,' I said, walking away from Frye and his officers, who fell in step. My driver was seated behind the wheel of the limo, Miss Hiss asleep in his arms.

'Looks like you have a friend,' I said as he lowered his window.

The driver grinned. 'Nice little cat. Wish I could keep her.'

'Why don't you?'

'Three dogs and a wife.'

'We'll take the cat,' Frye said.

'To where? The pound?'

'She'll be all right.'

'Absolutely not. I'll take her with me to the hotel.'

'Whatever you say.' There was fatigue in his voice.

'Do you know where I can buy cat food and litter this time of night?' I asked.

Frye turned to an officer. 'Go find a couple of bowls, litter, a litter box, and some cat food.'

'Huh?'

'Just do it,' Frye said. 'Bring it to ... what hotel are you at?'

'The Sheraton-Park Avenue.'

'Bring it there.'

'Yes, sir.'

'Thank you.'

My driver handed Miss Hiss to me. She purred, and I squeezed her. We went to the police car, photographers' strobes going off with every step.

'Get some sleep, Mrs Fletcher,' Frye said through the partially open window after Miss Hiss and I were settled in the backseat. 'If you need anything, call me directly.' He handed me a card that included his private telephone number.

'I want you to know, Commissioner Frye, that I don't like any of this.'

'Better than tripping over dead bodies.

Good night, Mrs Fletcher. Sleep tight.'

*   *   *

'Good morning, Mrs Fletcher,' a pleasant male voice said on the phone.

'Morning?' I looked at the watch I'd worn to bed. It was seven; I'd gotten to sleep at four.

'My name is Tom Detienne. I'm the hotel's assistant manager.'

I said in a thick, slurred voice, 'Yes?'

'Could I have a few minutes of your time this morning?'

'This morning?' I rubbed my eyes and sat up. 'I haven't had much sleep, Mr Detienne. When did you want to see me?'

'Whenever it's convenient for you.'

'I suppose if I get up now and take a shower—I need breakfast. Yes, I'm hungry. Would an hour be all right? Make it an hour and a half.'

'Eight-thirty will be fine. What would you like for breakfast? I'll put in the order personally.'

'That's kind of you.' I told him what I wanted.

'What time would you like it delivered, Mrs Fletcher?'

'Oh, eight.'

'It will be there at eight, and I'll come up at eight-thirty. Thank you.'

I stumbled out of bed, went to the bathroom,

122

and splashed cold water on my face. I looked at myself in the mirror: 'You look the way you feel, Jessica.' More water on my face and over my wrists, something my mother taught me when I was a child. The blood in the wrists is cooled and goes to the rest of the body, which helps wake you up. At least that's what she said. I have no idea whether there is any physiological truth to it, but it always seems to work.

I felt better after showering. At eight sharp, a bellhop arranged my breakfast on the desk near the window.

At eight-thirty, Mr Detienne arrived, a tall, handsome man with gray hair and horn-rimmed glasses. He wore a nicely tailored gray suit. 'Sorry to intrude upon you, Mrs Fletcher.'

'Don't be silly. My life has been nothing but intrusions since I arrived in New York. Please, sit down.'

Miss Hiss came from where she'd been sleeping on a couch and rubbed against his leg. He smiled and stroked her head. 'Nice cat,' he said.

'Her name is Miss Hiss. I hope you don't mind my keeping her here.' I'd arranged the water and food bowls, and litter pan in the bathroom and had created a bed from towels.

'No, that's fine,' he said. 'We don't allow pets under ordinary circumstances, but this is hardly ordinary.'

'Far from it,' I said.

Detienne seemed unsure, or unwilling to say what was on his mind. Finally, he looked up from highly polished shoes he'd been examining and said, 'Mrs Fletcher, this whole thing is getting out of hand. You've seen today's papers?'

'No, I haven't.'

He picked up the phone and instructed someone to bring up all the morning papers. He resumed his seat and said to me, 'The lobby is crawling with press. Two uniformed New York City policemen are sitting in chairs outside your door. The phones are ringing off their hooks with calls from other media inquiring about you. Mobile TV vans are lined up in front of the entrance, which keeps our guests from getting cabs. Guests are complaining. We have a lot of regulars who come here because we are a quiet oasis in the middle of Manhattan. That's no longer true, I'm afraid.'

I felt guilty and embarrassed. At the same time, I knew that none of this was my doing. Well, that wasn't entirely true. Seeing Waldo Morse shot on the street was certainly not my fault. But if I hadn't pursued the Joe Charles-Alphonse Rizzi-Susan Kale connection, I would not have ended up discovering her body in a loft on Crosby Street.

'I'm terribly sorry about this, Mr Detienne. I was staying with friends when all this broke, and I felt it wasn't fair to have them subjected to the chaos. Now, I guess I've done the same thing to you and your guests. I'll arrange to leave immediately.'

He shook his head. 'No, Mrs Fletcher. I'm not asking you to do that. We're honored to have someone of your stature staying with us. What I was going to suggest was that we move you to our penthouse suite on the roof. That would get you out of the main flow of hotel traffic. The suite has three bedrooms. Maybe your police protection could station themselves in one of them, or out on the roof. There's a lovely garden just outside the suite's patio doors, and you'll have a private elevator, and—'

'Put the police out in a garden in this weather?'

Detienne laughed. 'We've already discussed that and are willing to go to the expense and trouble of putting up a tent, and to use portable heating units to keep them warm. In other words, Mrs Fletcher, we'll go to any lengths to accommodate you, while at the same time accommodating our other guests. The move won't cost you any more.'

'That's very generous,' I said.

'Your bill is being paid by Buckley House, and we'll inform them, if you wish, that you'll be in the penthouse at no additional charge.'

'Wouldn't it be better if I just found another place to stay?'

'Wouldn't hear of it, Mrs Fletcher.' He

stood.

There was a knock on the door. Detienne answered and handed me the morning newspapers. The *Daily News* was on top. Its front page was a photograph of me exiting the building on Crosby Street at three o'clock that morning. The story began: *Famed mystery writer Jessica Fletcher, who witnessed the murder of the sidewalk Santa on Tuesday, discovered the body early this morning of a young woman named Susan Kale. Looks like Jessica Fletcher doesn't have to make up plots for her murder mysteries any longer. She can take all she needs from her real-life experiences.*

'This is awful,' I said.

'Very upsetting to you, I'm sure.'

Next came the *Post*. It had two photographs on the front page. One was of me climbing into the car provided by Commissioner Frye, Miss Hiss in my arms. The other was of the body bag containing Susan Kale's remains being loaded into a police ambulance. The *Post* headline read: ANOTHER REAL MURDER FOR JESSICA FLETCHER. The caption read: *Mystery writer Jessica Fletcher, in New York to promote her latest murder mystery, has been promoting real murder since her arrival. She witnessed the slaying of a sidewalk Santa on Fifth Avenue, and early this morning discovered the body of a young woman on Crosby Street.* Post *reporter Bobby Johnson, who has been following Ms. Fletcher's bloody trail, reports on Page Three.*

I tossed the *Post* on the floor along with the *News*, and scanned the front page of the *New York Times*. There was no mention of the events of a few hours ago but Detienne suggested I look at the first page of the Metro Section. There it was, a brief story that reported the death of Susan Kale. It went on to say that I had found the body, and was the one who'd witnessed the murder of the sidewalk Santa.

'Even the *Times*,' I sighed.

'I'll leave these with you,' Detienne said. 'When you head off for the day, I'll have our staff move you to the penthouse. Again, Mrs Fletcher, I hope this won't cause you any additional grief.'

I heard his words but didn't digest them. I finally realized he'd been speaking to me, looked at him, and said, 'Oh, my mind is elsewhere, which is probably good. Thank you for your courtesy. Please ask your staff to move Miss Hiss to the penthouse, too, and to take care that she doesn't get loose.'

'I understand,' he said. 'I have two cats of my own.'

When he was gone, I absently opened the *Post* to Page Three. Bobby Johnson was getting up in the world; there was a head shot of him along with photographs from the scene of Susan Kale's murder. My eyes sped over the page and stopped on a paragraph where a name popped out at me—Detective Alphonse

Rizzi. He'd given a statement to the press:

'The deceased, a Ms Susan Kale, was found dead in her apartment on Crosby Street. She was in the process of moving because there was no furniture in the apartment, and there were boxes containing her possessions. We have no leads at this time, but an initial examination of the body by an assistant medical examiner indicates that she was sexually assaulted, and that heavy traces of cocaine were found in her bloodstream.'

Impossible, I thought. The girl seemed perfectly lucid when we talked. I hadn't examined the body, but from what I could see she was fully clothed. She'd been beaten about the head, which undoubtedly caused her death.

I didn't see any signs of what Rizzi had said. And, I asked myself, why had he indicated that it was her apartment? Surely, he knew about her relationship with Joe Charles, and that Joe Charles lived there. He'd called and left a message on the answering machine confirming their eleven-o'clock rendezvous at Sweet Basil. Not only that, I had no doubt that he was aware that Waldo Morse was a friend of both Joe Charles and Susan Kale. None of that was mentioned in his statement.

Rizzi ended his comments to the press with:

'Unfortunately, a guest of our city, famous mystery writer Jessica Fletcher, had to be the one to discover the body. You'll recall that it was Mrs Fletcher who witnessed the shooting of the Santa Claus on Fifth Avenue on Tuesday. Mrs Fletcher

128

evidently happened upon the body purely by chance, but we are providing her with round-the-clock police protection for the duration of her stay in Manhattan.'

Ruth Lazzara called from the lobby. She was to accompany me to a book signing at a midtown store. 'Mrs Fletcher,' she said breathlessly, 'I can't believe what's happened to you. *Another* murder?'

'Afraid so, I think I'd better go home to Cabot Cove. If I stay much longer, your homicide rate will break all records.'

'Are you all right?' she asked. 'I mean, are you up to making appearances today?'

'I think so. I might as well. They don't murder people in bookstores, do they?' I was sorry at my feeble attempt to make light of what had happened. Somehow, it didn't lend itself to comedy high or low. 'I'll be down in a minute,' I said. 'But, I should warn you, Ruth, we'll have a couple of uniformed members of New York's finest with us every step of the way.'

'Maybe that's a good thing. There's plenty of press down here.'

'You'll steer me through them, I'm sure.'

Two policemen sat in the hall in straight-back chairs.

'Good morning,' I said.

'Good morning, ma'am.' As I started down the hall, they trailed after me. I stopped and turned. 'There really is no need for you to spend the day with me.'

'Orders, ma'am.'

'Yes, I suppose you have no choice in the matter. Well, come on. It's going to be a busy day.'

And tomorrow, too, I thought. Police escorts or not, I was going to Cabot Cove in the morning and I intended to make that trip alone.

CHAPTER THIRTEEN

When I returned to the hotel at five, I was personally escorted to the penthouse by Mr Detienne. It was a stunning suite of rooms on the top of the hotel. A sliding glass door led to the roof garden, a vast expanse of Astro Turf stretching to the roof's edge. Nothing was in bloom, of course, but dozens of evergreens in large wooden tubs and strung with hundreds of tiny white Christmas lights defined the area.

I'd insisted that the two policemen assigned to me take one of the inside rooms, rather than being banished to a tent. There was more to my decision than altruism. The suite was served by a private elevator, which seemed to be the only access to it. I asked Detienne whether there was another exit.

'There's a small elevator that goes down to the kitchen,' he said. 'It's on the other side of the roof. Why do you ask?'

'No special reason,' I said cheerily. 'Just my natural curiosity at work. I always look for entrances and exits wherever I stay, a habit I got into when placing my characters in different situations.'

He laughed. 'Always working, huh?'

'Afraid so. It goes with the territory of being a writer. As an author-friend of mine often says, "Everything gets used."'

After Detienne gave me a tour of the suite, I threw up my hands and said, 'This is absolutely lovely. Thank you so much.'

'My pleasure. Would you like me to make a dinner reservation for you tonight?'

'Goodness, no. As far as I know, I have the night off and intend to take full advantage of it—a long soak in a hot tub, a good book, asleep by nine.'

'Dinner in your room?'

'Splendid. I'll check the room-service menu and call down a little later.'

I walked him to the door that led to the interior hall and the suite's elevator. 'Might I ask you something, Mrs Fletcher?' he said.

'Of course.'

'I know the police are here for your protection, but do you feel secure having them in the suite with you?' My puzzled expression prompted him to add, 'They may be police, but you never know what kind of people they really are. I mean, a single woman sharing a suite

131

with two strange men could be—well, awkward.'

I smiled. 'I've thought of that, and I don't have any qualms. The bedroom they're staying in is certainly enough removed from mine, and has its own bath facilities. They know I need my privacy. Their door will be closed, and so will mine. But thank you for thinking of it. Good night, Mr Detienne. I'll be fine.'

I must admit that I was a little on edge as I soaked in the tub knowing that two strange men were in the next room. But I didn't dwell upon it. The luxurious pleasure of the hot water penetrating my skin was too delicious to let anything mitigate the experience.

I stayed in the tub for almost an hour. Shriveled, contented, and sleepy, I wrapped myself in a thick terry cloth robe provided by the hotel and placed my dinner order—shrimp cocktail, lamb chops cooked pink, fresh asparagus, a spinach salad, a raspberry tart, and a large pot of tea. It was scrumptious, and when I climbed into bed at precisely nine, Margaret Truman's latest capital crimes mystery on the pillow next to me, I felt as though I'd been transported to a gentler, kinder place, at least for this night. I could see through the windows that it was crystal clear outside. Stars twinkled in a black sky, like the lights on the evergreens. It was windy; the windowpanes rattled, which only added to my feeling of secure coziness.

I didn't leave a wake-up call because I didn't want the phone to ring. Instead, I set a tiny travel alarm I always carry with me and awoke at five to its faint, lilting chime. I quickly turned it off, got out of bed, crossed the carpeted room to the closed door, and pressed an ear to it. A television was playing in the room assigned to the officers. I couldn't make out what they were watching, but it didn't matter. Any sound would help.

I dressed in casual clothing—slacks, sweater, sneakers—then went to the bathroom where my black wig and sunglasses were on the vanity. I put them on and checked myself in the mirror. Hopefully, the disguise wouldn't be necessary. The officers seemed content watching Saturday morning fare on TV, and their replacements wouldn't arrive until seven. By then, I'd be long gone.

I buttoned my coat, pulled the collar up around my chin and neck, picked up a small bag I'd packed the night before, carefully opened my door, and waited. The sound of the TV was louder now that my door wasn't a barrier to it. One of the officers laughed; they were watching a cartoon. Thank you Nickelodeon.

I stepped into the foyer that connected the suite's bedrooms, pressed my door shut, and went through the living room to the sliding doors. I undid the latch, slid the doors open just enough for me to squeeze through, and

133

closed them.

The wind was still blowing fiercely; hopefully, it wouldn't disrupt flights out of New York's airports. It was still dark, but the tiny lights on the trees gave off enough illumination for me to make my way.

I moved toward the back of the garden and up steps into an area used for summer concerts. I turned right again until reaching the rear of the hotel and the door Detienne had mentioned. It hadn't occurred to me that it might be locked. It was. I noticed a small button next to it and pressed, heard a ringing from far below and the groan of an ascending elevator. The door opened and a young Hispanic kitchen worker dressed in whites faced me.

'I'm Jessica Fletcher, the mystery writer. I'm staying in the penthouse suite and am researching different ways my characters might move through the hotel. Please take me down to the kitchen.' I added, 'Mr Detienne, the assistant manager, knows about this.'

He either didn't understand much English, or the sight of a ridiculous-looking, windblown woman standing outside at five-thirty in the morning was too much of a shock. He didn't argue, simply stepped aside. I got into the elevator and rode it down to the kitchen where I received more quizzical stares. I ignored them and went through swinging doors into the empty main dining room, and to an exit onto

Thirty-seventh Street. To my delight, a cab sat at the curb, motor running, driver snoozing. I knocked on the window; he awoke with a start. 'LaGuardia Airport,' I said through the window. He unlocked the curbside passenger door, and I slid into the seat. 'The Delta Shuttle.'

As we headed for the airport, I removed my wig and sunglasses, an action the driver noticed in his rearview mirror. 'I just came from a costume party,' I said pleasantly.

'Must have been a hell of a party,' he commented.

'Oh, it certainly was. It's still going on.' I stuffed the paraphernalia into my bag.

The driver kept glancing at me in the mirror all the way to the airport. Maybe I should have continued to wear my disguise. If he recognized me from all the pictures in the newspapers, it could jeopardize my determination to leave the city unnoticed. As it turned out, he didn't say another word.

As I crossed the nearly deserted terminal, I passed a newsstand on which all three New York papers were prominently displayed. There I was again on the front page of two of them. I detoured to a lady's room where I put on my wig and sunglasses, then went to the counter and bought my ticket to Boston— under my real name, the name on my charge card.

'You're the famous writer,' the pretty blond

ticket agent said.

I glanced left and right before leaning across the counter and whispering, 'Yes, but I prefer to keep it quiet today.'

She handed me my boarding pass, wished me a pleasant flight, and whispered, 'Your secret is safe with me, Mrs Fletcher.'

The 727's passenger compartment was sparsely populated. Most of my fellow-passengers read the *Times*, but a young man and woman across the aisle perused their individual copies of the *Post*. I'd intended to remove the uncomfortable wig once we were airborne, but thought better of it. I settled in my seat and, in what seemed only minutes, the captain announced we were beginning our descent into Logan Airport.

I smiled contentedly. It had worked even better than I'd hoped. No hitches, no glitches. Way to go, Jess.

Brimming with confidence, I stashed my wig and sunglasses and left the aircraft with my head high. New York City didn't exist. I was going home. I had only one moment of concern. As I reached the terminal's main entrance and looked for Jed Richardson, an unmarked green sedan barreled up to the entrance and two men jumped out. Police, I thought, turning away. Could they be looking for me? Impossible. I'd only been gone a few hours.

I looked over my shoulder and saw them run

inside the terminal. Then, I heard Jed Richardson's loud, gravelly voice yell, 'Jessica. Over here.'

Not so loud! Jed stood next to a taxi. After a final glance at the terminal doors—the two men had disappeared inside—I quickly crossed the road.

'Sight for sore eyes,' Jed said, an infectious grin on his round, tanned, deeply creased face. He wore a battered leather aviator's jacket, a white silk scarf around his neck, and a blue peaked cap with *Jed's Flying Service* emblazoned on it.

'Where's your plane?' I asked.

'Over at private aviation. I got me this cab.' The driver, an older man with a large, bulbous nose, did not look happy that we were standing there talking. I suggested we get going. 'You bet,' Jed said. 'Looks like we got us a serious weather front coming through. The sooner we get off, the better.'

Our driver complained for the duration of the short trip to the private aviation area: 'I could have had a fare into the city,' he said more than once. To which Jed replied: 'And we could have ended up with a pleasant driver.'

He dropped us next to a hangar. I went through my usual debate of whether to tip him a lot to compensate for the short trip, or to tip him little for his rudeness. My choice fell somewhere in between. He looked at the money I handed him, shrugged, and drove off.

'Damn big-city attitude,' Jed said.

'You should visit New York,' I said.

'No thanks. Boston's as big as I ever want to visit. Don't much like Bangor, either, no more. Come on, Jessica. Let's get outta here.'

We walked to Jed's single-engine Cessna 185 Skywagon, which was parked in a row of other small planes. Jed also owned two twin-engine aircraft, and I wished he'd brought one of them. Having to depend only upon one engine increased my general nervousness about flying.

'Be the last flight in this honey,' Jed said, patting the small plane's wing. 'Got a fella going to pick it up next week. Got a right good price for it.'

'Good,' I said. I was anxious to get inside; the open area in which we stood was like a wind tunnel, its chilled air biting into my cheeks. On the other hand, getting in meant taking off. No backing out now. Jed was there because I'd asked him to be, and I certainly trusted his flying ability. He'd spent years as a top-rated commercial pilot before opening his own small airline.

I settled into the right-hand seat, and Jed got into the left. The engine turned over smoothly, and we were soon taxiing toward the operative runway that windy, cold December morning in Boston. Jed invited me to put on an extra set of headphones in order to hear the dialogue between him and the controller. I had trouble making out their words, but they seemed to

138

know precisely what each other was saying. We were told there were two commercial airline jets cleared to take off before us. Jed leaned over to me and said, 'Got to keep our distance from those babies. Damn vortex coming off their wings, and the thrust from their engines could blow us over like a piece 'a paper.'

I laughed nervously: 'Yes, by all means, Jed. Let's keep our distance.'

I watched the two commercial jets take off and formed the same question I always did— how can anything that big get off the ground?

We were instructed to hold because a plane was landing. After it had, Jed received permission to take his position on the active runway. 'Cessna six seven-A cleared for takeoff,' the controller said.

'Roger, Cessna six-seven-A rolling,' Jed replied. He pushed the throttle forward, the engine roared to maximum life, and we bounced down the seemingly endless strip of concrete, the wind doing its best to blow us off to the side. We hadn't gone very far when Jed pulled back on the yoke and the plane waffled into the air. The controller instructed him to make a right turn and to climb on an assigned compass heading until reaching two thousand feet.

I looked out my window and saw the city of Boston slide away beneath me. I had to admit that while I was still nervous—my stomach confirmed that—I also found it exhilarating. I looked through the front window at the blur of the whirling propeller. Just keep spinning.

We achieved Jed's requested cruising altitude of eight thousand feet, and the small plane moved smoothly through the air. He tapped me on the shoulder and pointed to his left. 'There's that front I told you about, Jess.' I followed the direction of his finger and saw a wall of black clouds. 'See up on top of that big one over there? See how it's shaped like an anvil?'

'Yes.'

'Big storm clouds always get that shape on top. We'll stay plenty clear of that baby. Could toss us about like a tennis ball, snap the wings right off.'

Stop talking about the terrible things that can happen to us, I thought. I held my tongue. Jed loved flying and took pride in pointing out such things to his passengers. Still . . .

We gave wide berth to all the unsettled weather enroute, and Jed eventually pointed out Cabot Cove to me. Try as I did, I couldn't distinguish it from any of the other towns we'd flown over; thousands of hours of viewing things from the air develop a different visual acuity in pilots, I suppose.

'There's the runway,' Jed said.

I squinted. 'Where?'

He laughed. 'No need for you to see it, Jess. Just so long as I do.'

Our relatively smooth flight had become

140

bumpy. The small plane lurched up and down, left and right, and we once dropped what seemed like a thousand feet, although I suppose it wasn't that far. Jed saw the frightened expression on my face and patted my knee. 'Always gets rougher down near the ground,' he said. 'Not to worry.'

He approached the runway, which I could see clearly now, on an angle. When we were almost over one end of it, Jed turned the aircraft to the right and we flew parallel to the concrete strip on our left. 'Got a left-hand landing pattern here,' he said. 'Flyin' downwind now. Always land into the wind, so we'll take a left when we get to the end, then take another left and smack into it.'

'Interesting,' I said.

Then it happened, suddenly and without fanfare. I didn't notice the propeller stop but I certainly heard the terminal cough from the engine.

'What's the matter?' I asked.

'Damn carb heat control acting up again. Been havin' trouble all winter. Promised to fix it before the fella who bought it picks it up next week.'

There was silence now, the only sound a whoosh of air passing the cockpit. The prop was dead. So was the engine.

'What do we do now?' I asked, picturing us pitching nose-first into the woods.

'Got to dead-stick her,' Jed said, his voice as

calm as usual.

'But we don't have an engine.'

'Don't need one. We'll just glide ourselves right on down.'

Jed never varied from his planned approach. It seemed to me at the last minute that we were getting dangerously close to the ground, but we crossed the end of the runway and, within seconds, touched down for a perfect landing.

'Biggest trouble is gettin' this thing to the hangar,' Jed said as he reached a taxiway using the plane's remaining forward momentum. We came to a stop halfway between the runway and hangar. 'See if I can raise anybody in Unicom,' he said, speaking into the handheld microphone. There was no answer. 'Guess Joe Harley ain't arrived yet. You sit tight, Jess.'

I watched him trudge toward the hangar that also served as the airport office. No engine meant no cabin heat, and I began to shiver. But my spirits picked up when I saw Jed leave the hangar accompanied by two familiar faces, Seth Hazlitt and Sheriff Morton Metzger. I opened my door and was outside when they arrived. After hugs all around, Jed said, 'Let's go. This baby won't move on her own.'

I got behind one wing with Seth, and Jed and Morton took the other. Together, we pushed the plane to the hangar.

'Sorry about that, Jess,' Jed said. 'Should of fixed that damn carb heat a long time ago.'

'You'd better fix it before your buyer

arrives,' I said. 'Actually, it was kind of exciting. I felt like I was in a glider.'

'That's because you were. Call any time you need another ride.'

'That will be tomorrow,' I said. 'Can you fly me back to Boston?'

'Ayuh. What time you plannin' on leavin'?'

'I have to be back in New York City by noon. I suppose I should take the nine-thirty shuttle.'

We set a time to depart Cabot Cove, and I went with Seth and Morton to where Morton's squad car waited. 'I didn't expect to see you here,' I told him.

Metzger, who wore a green down coat with a fake fur collar with his tan uniform, earmuffs, and a large Stetson hat, said, 'Had nothin' else to do, Jessica.' He started the engine. 'Where to?'

'Nancy Morse's house.'

Mort looked at me. I was in front with him, Seth in the back. 'What are we goin' there for?' Metzger asked.

'I have to speak with her about something. Actually, I have some unpleasant news to deliver.'

'About Waldo?' Metzger said.

'Yes. I assume Seth told you.'

Metzger looked over his shoulder. 'Can't say he told me everything, but enough for me to get the gist.'

The Morse house was in a lovely community ten miles north of Cabot Cove Center. Each

143

house was nestled into its own unique natural setting of rocks and trees. The Morse house was especially nice because it was poised on a rise that gave it the development's highest vantage point. A steep, narrow road led up to the driveway; you couldn't see the house until you were almost upon it. This day, it was also hidden behind a large moving van.

We parked in front of the truck and walked to where the driveway began. From there, I could see a figure passing back and forth behind a large picture window. I assumed it was Nancy. 'Coming with me?' I asked my companions.

'Might as well,' Seth said. 'Judgin' from this truck, you didn't get here any too soon.'

We walked three abreast up the driveway and paused in front of the entrance to the house. 'Here goes,' I said. I climbed the steps and, as I reached for the doorbell, the door opened and Nancy Morse looked down at me.

'Hello, Nancy. I'm Jessica Fletcher.'

She scrutinized me closely. When she accepted that I was who I claimed to be, she turned her attention to Seth and Morton.

'Mornin', Mrs Morse,' Seth said. Mort grunted and tipped his Stetson.

'What do you want?' Nancy asked.

'Just a little time to talk,' I said pleasantly. 'May we come in?'

Two moving men carrying a couch came up behind Nancy and excused themselves. They passed, and I repeated my request.

'Can't you see I'm busy?' Nancy said.

'Gracious, yes. I certainly can see that. I can't imagine anything more disruptive than moving. Where are you going?'

She started to answer, but her words trailed off as an angry expression crossed her face. 'Please. Leave me alone,' she said.

'Nancy, I don't wish to cause you any problems, but I've flown here this morning from New York because I have something important to tell you.'

Her eyes widened, and she placed her hands on her hips. 'So, tell me and let me get out of here.'

'Nancy, Waldo is dead. He's been murdered.'

'I know.'

'You do? Who told you?'

'It doesn't matter. If that's why you came here, you wasted a trip.'

I looked closely at her and saw two things— the gradual erosion of the youthful, blond beauty she'd been as a high school cheerleader, and the beginnings of an older woman of whom life was beginning to take advantage. Behind her defiant, angry mask was a soft vulnerability that she worked hard to keep in the background. I said, 'Nancy, if you will give me just ten minutes, I promise we'll get out of your hair for good. But I *witnessed* Waldo's murder. I have some questions. Please, if you'll just give me—'

She turned and went into the house, the door still open. The moving men returned and entered. Seth, Mort, and I went right along with them.

Although the house was in disarray because of the move, the interior was every bit as beautiful as the exterior. The living room was massive and dominated by a huge natural stone fireplace that spanned an entire wall. An Indian family could have cooked in it. Lived in it.

'Jess, maybe we should . . .' Seth said.

'No. She has to talk to me.'

I didn't know where Nancy had gone so I went through the first open door, which led to the kitchen. All the appliances were restaurant grade and size. Another door from it led to a large deck overlooking a lavishly landscaped yard. I was about to retrace my steps to the living room when Nancy suddenly appeared. 'How dare you come in here,' she said.

I extended my hands in a gesture of pleading. 'Nancy, I not only saw Waldo murdered, I discovered the body yesterday of a young woman with whom he was involved. She also was murdered. I know these two horrible incidents are related.'

'So?'

'So, that means that *your* life could be in danger.'

Her laugh was scornful. 'Don't you think I

146

already know that? Why the hell do you think we're moving, leaving this beautiful house, yanking the kids out of good schools? Come on, Mrs Fletcher, give me a break. Stick to writing murder mysteries and leave us real people alone.'

Her words stung but I pressed on. 'Do you remember a young man from Cabot Cove named Joe Charles?'

'No.'

I started to ask another question but she turned on Seth and Morton. 'Why are you two standing there gawking? You have no right in here. I haven't done anything wrong.'

I wanted to keep her talking. If the presence of Seth and Morton upset her, I'd stand a better chance if they left. They knew what I was thinking, excused themselves, and departed, leaving Nancy and me alone in the kitchen. 'Joe Charles was a musician,' I said. 'His real name when he was going to high school was Johnson. They called him Junior. Does that ring a bell?'

She said, 'Yes, I think I remember somebody with that name.'

'Have you seen him since he departed Cabot Cove? He left to make a career in music.'

'I don't know anything about Junior Johnson, or this Joe Charles.'

'The reason I ask, Nancy, is that Joe Charles and Waldo were friendly in New York. In fact, they lived together, at least some of the time. It was in Joe Charles's apartment that this young

147

woman, Susan Kale, was murdered. Joe Charles has disappeared, and quite suddenly.' I sighed, shook my head, and leaned against a large center island above which copper pots and pans hung. 'I know there's a connection between all of this, Nancy, and I came here hoping you might help me make that connection. Did you have any contact with Waldo after he went into the witness protection program?'

'Damn it, Mrs Fletcher, don't you ever get the hint? Of course I never heard from Waldo. That's the idea of the program. People disappear in it, leaving everybody else swinging in the wind.'

'But he must have sent you money.' I extended my arms to take in the kitchen. 'Surely, someone from the government supported you.'

'That is between me and the government.'

'Yes, I suppose that's the way it must be. Still, it's hard for me to conceive of a husband and father never making contact with his family again.'

'That's your problem,' she said.

'It's become my problem only because I witnessed Waldo's murder. Waldo was working as a volunteer Santa Claus on Fifth Avenue when he was shot. Do you have any idea why he might have taken such a visible job, considering his need to remain in hiding from the drug dealers he turned in?'

'Not so visible. Santa Claus wears a beard, doesn't he?'

'Not a very good one. Have you ever heard from any of the drug dealers who went to jail as a result of Waldo's testimony?'

She snickered. 'If I had, Mrs Fletcher, I wouldn't be standing in this kitchen talking to you. They don't play by the same rules as the rest of the world.'

'But it would seem to me that they would know Waldo had a family. From what I hear about the way they do business, they wouldn't hesitate to take out their anger on the family of an informer.'

'Look, Mrs Fletcher, I know I've been rude and I apologize for that. I've been under a tremendous strain.'

'I understand,' I said. 'I dread the day I ever have to move.'

'I'm talking about the strain of having a husband leave me and his children, then be accused of smuggling drugs, and then testify against the others he was involved with in return for disappearing, a new life, one that didn't include me or the kids. It has hurt them terribly. I ask forgiveness every day for that.'

'It seems Waldo's the one who should ask for forgiveness.'

'That wasn't Waldo's nature. Excuse me. I need to talk to the movers.'

Alone in the kitchen, I went to the window and looked outside. The movers were carrying a large dresser to the truck. Then, I heard a voice from inside the house. A man's voice. Nancy said something. They both sounded angry. I was tempted to go in search of them, but thought better of it. Nancy was upset enough. Who was the man? I had a hunch about that.

I meandered the kitchen's perimeter. Everything was obviously expensive; no cost had been spared to create a stunning and functional kitchen. On one countertop in the corner was a pad of lined, yellow legal-size paper. I glanced down at the first page. Nancy had been writing a letter using a blue ballpoint pen that rested on the pad. It started with that day's date; it began, 'To whom it may concern.' I started to read the first paragraph when she returned to the kitchen, saw what I was doing, and tore off the pages.

'It's possible you'll hear from Junior Johnson, also known as Joe Charles,' I said.

'I doubt that. No one is going to know where we've gone.'

'That may be your goal, Nancy, but it's not easy to completely disappear. My point is that if you should hear from him, I would appreciate knowing about it. Believe me, this is not to satisfy my idle curiosity. It has to do with murder ... *two* murders ... and I've found myself more involved with both than I'd like to be.'

'I'll let you know if I hear from him,' she

said.

'Thank you. If you can't reach me—I'll be in New York through the new year—you can call Dr Hazlitt, or Sheriff Metzger.'

'Sure.'

I knew I had overstayed my welcome and that she was getting ready again to tell me to leave. I would spare her that. 'Thank you for talking to me, Nancy. I wish you and the children well wherever you go. Where are the children?'

'With my mother.'

Instead of accompanying me from the kitchen, she left by herself. I hesitated, then tore off a few sheets of paper from the yellow pad, leaving enough pages so that it wouldn't be noticed. I put them under my coat, walked through the living room, and rejoined Seth and Morton in the driveway.

'You should have gotten in the car and used the heater,' I said. 'You both look frozen.'

'Not so bad with the sun shinin',' Seth said, looking up and squinting into a brilliant blue sky. 'Nancy Morse certainly was some ugly.'

'I feel sorry for her,' I said.

'Looks like the storm they forecast missed us,' Morton said.

'And a good thing it has,' I said. 'Know what I want to do? I would like to go to my house, get a fire going, and have some clam pie. Is Charlene Sassi still making pies and selling them?'

'Sure is.'

'Splendid. Let's stop at her house and get some. The treat's on me.'

I bought the last two clam pies Charlene had to sell, and we headed for my place. I felt like a little girl anticipating arrival at a special amusement park. I couldn't wait to be in my own home again, to sit around the table with friends, and enjoy Charlene's clam pie that someone once described as 'like going to heaven.'

'Home! It looks wonderful,' I said as Mort pulled into my driveway. Joseph, a mildly retarded gentleman who made a pretty good living around town as a handyman, had shoveled my driveway and walk. Whenever I was away, he also checked on the house every day to make sure that the heat, which I left on a low setting, was still on, and took in my mail and newspapers.

I got out of the car and headed for the front door.

'Don't slip,' Seth said. I looked down, saw the icy patch to which he was referring, skirted it, fumbled for keys in my purse, and opened the door. I stood in the middle of the living room and did a clumsy pirouette. 'Look. Joseph has put wood in the fireplace. Put a match to it, Seth, while I set the table.'

A half hour later we enthusiastically dug into the pies. 'Mort,' I said between bites, 'I heard the news about Parker Brothers being

152

interested in your game.'

'Haven't heard another word from them, so I don't get my hopes up. I suppose they get lots of people like me inventing games and sending them to them, bein' the biggest and all.'

'But your game is really very good,' I said. 'Take it from a mystery writer.'

Seth sat back, dabbed at his mouth with a napkin, and patted his sizable belly. 'So, Jessica Fletcher, you got your chance to talk to Nancy Morse. Didn't seem to me like she was likely to be any help.'

'It looks that way, Seth, but I haven't had a chance to digest what she said.'

'How about fillin' us in on everything's been happening to you down in New York,' Mort said, taking another serving.

'I wouldn't even know where to begin. Actually, I'm not supposed to be here.'

'That young lady you found?' Seth asked.

'Yes. You know about that?'

'Been on the radio this mornin'.'

I sighed and shook my head. 'Because of finding that young woman's body, I was prohibited from leaving New York.'

'Don't seem right,' Metzger said. 'No crime in findin' a body. Causin' one's another matter.'

'How did you manage to leave?' Hazlitt asked.

'I'll show you.' I went to the bedroom, put on the wig and sunglasses, and returned to the dining room. 'Ta da,' I sang, assuming a silly model's pose.

'Who's that lady?' Seth asked Mort. They laughed heartily.

'Where did Jessica go?' Mort said, playing into the banter.

'Effective, huh?' I said.

'You look like one of those New York City cabaret singers,' Mort said.

'I hope so. Just as long as I didn't look like a mystery writer named Jessica Fletcher.' I pulled off the wig and glasses, and started to tell them how I'd managed to elude the New York patrolmen assigned to my suite. I didn't get very far. An automobile pulled into the driveway, doors opened, slammed shut, and footsteps were heard approaching the front door.

'Looks like you got company, Jess,' Seth said.

'I can't imagine who. Did you tell anyone I was coming home?'

'Nope,' Seth said. 'Well, a few folks, but I was pretty choosy about it.'

I threw my physician friend a skeptical glance as someone knocked.

'You sit,' Mort said, heading for the door. 'I'll get it.'

I couldn't hear what the man said to Mort, but I did hear my name. I raised eyebrows at Seth, and we joined them.

'Jessica Fletcher?' the man said. Another man stood directly behind him. They were straight out of central casting—police.

'Yes.'

'I'm Detective Pehanich, N.Y.P.D.' He flashed a badge at me. 'This is Detective Taylor.'

'Yes?'

'I'm afraid I'll have to ask you to come with us, Mrs Fletcher.'

'Why? I haven't done anything.'

'We have a warrant for your arrest.'

'On what charge?'

'Leaving the scene of a crime as a material witness.'

I couldn't help but laugh. 'That's nonsense,' I said. 'I'm coming back in the morning. I just left the city to—'

'Mrs Fletcher, please don't give us a hard time.'

Mort Metzger pulled himself up to full height and stepped between me and Pehanich. 'I'm Morton Metzger, sheriff of Cabot Cove,' he said with authority. 'Let me see that warrant.'

Pehanich handed it to Metzger, who took glasses from his pocket, perched them on his nose, and studied the paper carefully. He turned to me and said, 'Appears to be in order, Jess.'

'Could we get going, Mrs Fletcher,' Taylor said. 'If we leave now, we can catch the last flight out of Bangor.'

'Were you the gentlemen at Logan Airport

155

this morning?'

'No, ma'am. They were Boston police. Somebody from New York called them when they discovered you missing.'

I sighed. 'Your efficiency impresses me.'

'Please, ma'am. It's cold. We'd like to get back. The holidays and all.'

'Yes, the holidays,' I said wistfully. 'The holidays.'

Mort Metzger said, 'You don't have to go with them, Jess. We can fight extradition.'

'Hey, Sheriff, cool it,' Detective Taylor said. 'She's wanted back in New York as a witness, not 'cause she killed anybody.'

'Thank you very much,' I said.

'I mean it, Jess,' Mort said. 'We'll buzz up Cal Simons right now.' Simons was Cabot Cove's leading attorney.

'No, Morton, that won't be necessary. I was going back anyway and might as well have company.' I said to the detectives, 'Please come in and enjoy the fire while I clean up the dishes. There might even be some food left. We were enjoying clam pie.'

'No thank you, ma'am,' Pehanich said, 'but we will come inside. Please hurry. We don't want to miss that flight.'

I indicated to Seth that I wanted him to follow me into the kitchen. The moment we got there I whispered, 'Do me a favor. Go back to Nancy Morse's house and see if there's a young man with her. Don't let her see you. Stay out on the road and just watch.'

I quickly described the adult Junior Johnson, a.k.a. Joe Charles.

'What do I do if I see him?'

'Tell me the next time we talk.'

I sensed the presence of one of the detectives in the doorway and rinsed a dish.

'Please, Mrs Fletcher.'

'Of course. Sorry. I'm ready.'

I was led to the rental car the detectives had driven from Bangor Airport.

'No cuffs,' Mort Metzger said.

The detectives looked at him strangely. Taylor said, 'No, no cuffs, Sheriff. Nice town you have here.' He then said to me, 'My wife is a big fan, Mrs Fletcher. I wondered maybe you could autograph a book to her. Her name is Lynn.'

'Sure,' I said, climbing into the backseat. 'And let me have your mother-in-law's name, too. I'm sure she'd enjoy a copy.'

CHAPTER FOURTEEN

'Hard for me to believe, Mrs Fletcher, but that's what they say. You're a suspect in the murder of the Kale girl.'

The voice delivering this weighty message was Sergeant Dennis Murphy, one of New York's saintly Irish cops who would have made a far better Santa Claus than Waldo Morse had. He'd been assigned to me the minute I was spirited into the precinct by my two bounty hunters, and we sat in a small holding cell just beyond the booking area.

'Am I officially a suspect?' I asked, attempting to sound unconcerned.

'No. Just what I hear, ma'am. A shocker, I'd say. You, the world's most famous mystery writer—and obviously a fine lady, too—dragged into this tawdry affair. Must be a mistake is all I can figure.'

'Yes, there must be. It's preposterous. I found her. I didn't kill her.'

'I'm sure it will all be straightened out in short order. Sometimes when they don't have any leads, they . . .'

'. . . They accuse the closest, easiest person?' I said, finishing his thought. 'I have a problem with that logic.'

Murphy shrugged. I poised to deliver a speech about the absurdity of that approach to crime solving, but didn't. It would have been lost on him. Besides, he'd been extremely courteous and solicitous, even allowing me to use the phone before entering my confines. I'd made two calls, the first to Vaughan Buckley. My timing was good, considering it was Saturday night; I caught him as he and Olga were preparing to leave for dinner. He told me to sit tight and that he'd be there as soon as he could, hopefully with a lawyer named Winter, who, he claimed, was the city's best criminal attorney.

My second call was collect to Seth Hazlitt in Cabot Cove to let him know I'd arrived safely. My timing was good with that call, too. He and Mort Metzger were waiting to be picked up by Jed Richardson, who would fly them to Boston where they would catch the next available flight to New York.

'Please don't, Seth. I'm fine. I spoke with Vaughan Buckley, and he said—'

'Save your breath, Jessica. Mort and I had a meeting soon's those gorillas took you away. We decided our place was at your side.'

'But if you come, you'll have to . . .'

'Not another word. We'll head straight for that Park Avenue Hotel you're stayin' in. Be there as soon as we can.'

I stopped trying to dissuade them. They'd show up whether I wanted them to or not. Seeing them would be comforting, of course. But they could also add another complication, as had happened a year ago when they flew to London to 'comfort me' during the investigation of Marjorie Ainsworth's murder. Neither of these dear friends was at home in large cities, and their penchant for getting into trouble when away from their familiar, secure Cabot Cove was only slightly less than astounding.

But I should be the last one to talk about finding trouble in strange big cities. There I was sitting in a holding cell in N.Y.P.D. headquarters as a material witness to one murder and, as I'd just learned, a murder suspect in another. Time to stop worrying about others and to start worrying about myself. As absurd as I found the entire situation, the ramifications could be serious.

That realization turned the stuffy, hot cell into a refrigerator for me. I wrapped my arms about myself and waited for what would happen next.

Which was the arrival of Police Commissioner Ferdinand Frye. He nodded for Murphy to leave. When we were alone, Frye leaned against the bars and slowly shook his head. Then he smiled. 'What are we going to do with Jessica Fletcher?' he asked.

'My first suggestion is to let me out of here immediately.'

'Of course. That's why I'm here, to see that you leave without further delay.'

I stood and straightened my skirt. 'They took my coat,' I said.

'We'll get your coat, Mrs Fletcher. But before we do, and before you leave, there's the question of where you'll be going.'

'Pardon?'

'I want you out of this city.'

'And I would like very much to get out of this city, Commissioner Frye. My visit has not been what you would call festive and gay. But I have an obligation to see through my book promotion activities. I owe that to my publisher.'

'I'm sure Mr Buckley would understand if you cut it short. He must know how much you'd like to be home for the holidays. There's no place like it, as the song says.'

'True,' I said. 'And the contemplation of going home is more delicious than you could ever imagine. But no, I intend to stay as long as necessary to fulfill my obligations. My coat please.'

The wide, perpetual smile faded, replaced by a slash for a mouth and hard, dark eyes. He pushed away from the bars and closed the gap between us. 'Mrs Fletcher,' he said in the measured tones of an impatient schoolteacher explaining something to an especially dense student, 'your presence seriously hampers my ability to solve two murders. Your involvement in them, as coincidental as it might be, has created a media circus. If I didn't have faith in your integrity, I'd wonder whether it's all been designed to help sell your books.'

'I assure you that's not the case.'

'Of course it isn't. But you're in my way. I don't like it when people get in my way, Mrs Fletcher.'

'Fair enough,' I said. 'I'll do everything within my power to stay out of your way. But now I want to leave here, return to my hotel, and go to bed. I'm very tired.'

Footsteps sounded outside the cell, and

Vaughan suddenly appeared. With him was a short, squat man wearing a black cashmere overcoat and black astrakhan hat. 'Jessica,' Buckley said. 'How could they have put you in a cell like this?'

'I was just leaving,' I said, smiling sweetly at Commissioner Frye.

'What is she charged with?' Winter asked Frye. He might have been short, but his voice was tall.

'Nothing, Jerry,' Frye responded. 'How've you been?'

Winter ignored the pleasantry. 'Then why was she detained?' he asked.

'Mrs Fletcher is—*was* a material witness to murder.'

'As well as a suspect in another murder,' I interjected.

'That's ridiculous,' Buckley said.

'What she might be damn soon, Commissioner,' Winter said, 'is the plaintiff in a suit against you and the city.'

'As you wish,' Frye said. 'I suggest we all go home.'

'I went home,' I said, feeling my adrenaline surge. 'But you brought me back.'

'Back from where?' Buckley asked.

'Cabot Cove.'

'I didn't know you were going home, Jess.'

'It was my secret, at least for a few hours. May I?' Frye stepped back to allow me to exit. I turned and asked, 'Do your police have an unusually high number of sick days each year?'

'What?'

'There's no air in this building. Very unhealthy.'

'Thank you for pointing it out to me.'

Frye joined us as we walked to the front door. 'By the way, Mrs Fletcher,' he said, 'since you insist upon staying in New York, you're on your own. I'm canceling your police escort, effective immediately.'

'Frankly, that's good news,' I said. 'Thank you for your courtesies, Commissioner. Perhaps we'll meet again.' I extended my hand. As he took it, his winsome smile returned.

'It's been a pleasure,' he said.

'I'd like to say the same, but I really can't. Nothing personal.'

'Nothing personal when she files suit, either,' Winter said, a long black cigar clenched in his teeth.

'I somehow don't see Mrs Fletcher as the litigious type,' Frye said. 'But do whatever you think is right. Good night.'

As we watched Frye climb into the back of his limo and speed off, I drew a series of deep breaths. It was a cold, clear night. Overhead, thousands of jewellike white stars were displayed on a black scrim. Buckley said, 'I should have introduced you. Jerry Winter, Jessica Fletcher.'

Winter grunted something, reached in his pocket, and handed me his card. 'Monday morning at ten, my office.'

'Why?'

'To start the action against the city.'

I laughed. 'I'm afraid Commissioner Frye was right,' I said. 'I'm not litigious.'

'Suit yourself, Mrs Fletcher, but you've got this city where you want it. Well, whatever you decide to do, I'm glad I could help you out tonight. Lucky Vaughan caught me. I was heading out of town for the weekend.'

Help me out? I wondered. What did he do? Would he send a bill?

'He wouldn't send me a bill, would he?' I asked Vaughan after Winter had departed.

'He'd better not. If he does, I won't publish his next book. Look, Jess, I think this has gone far enough, you getting involved in *real* murder. Come on. We'll check you out of the hotel and move you back in with us. You talk to no one, no press, no cops, only book people. I'll instruct Ruth Lazzara to ease up on the schedule, focus only upon major media.'

I said I would think about it, but that I wanted that night in my suite to sleep away everything that had happened over the past twenty-four hours.

'Fine,' he said. 'But once you've done that, Olga and I want you back at the apartment.'

'Let me sleep on it, Vaughan. And thanks for being such a dear.' He drove me to the hotel, reiterated his wishes, wished me pleasant dreams, and drove off, leaving me to enter the empty lobby, dart into the elevator, ride it to the penthouse, and fling open the door. No room has ever looked more inviting—except for the flashing light on my telephone. A sign I'd left on my bathroom door, 'DO NOT OPEN! ATTACK CAT INSIDE,' was still there. I opened the door and Miss Hiss undulated through the opening, brushed against my leg, and wandered into the living room.

I called the desk and was given thirteen messages, most from media. Two were from Bobby Johnson, who invited me for brunch the next day, Sunday.

Sunday!

The press conference. A message left by what the hotel operator termed 'a frantic woman,' Ruth Lazzara, informed me that the conference would be held at three at the Plaza. The thought of it was depressing, but I had to go through with it. Lazzara didn't know anything about my having left the city and the ensuing madness. I returned her call; thankfully I reached her answering machine on which her frantic voice urged callers to leave a message. Which I did; I'd be there with bows on.

There was also a message from Seth and Morton. They'd called from the airport and would be at the hotel within the hour. I smiled. They'd be here in an hour provided the cab driver didn't bring them via Philadelphia.

Their pending arrival ruled out any long nap

so I showered, changed into slightly more dressy clothes, and waited for their next call. It came exactly an hour later. They'd checked in and were downstairs in the Judges' Chambers, the hotel bar.

'Gorry, you look like death,' Seth said when I joined them.

'Thank you for that vote of confidence, Seth.'

'No offense, Jessica, but the bloom is gone from your cheeks. I don't wonder. No one in this city has bloom on their cheeks. Just gray circles under their eyes.'

'It isn't *that* bad,' I said in defense. 'New York is actually a nice place—once you get used to it. It grows on you.'

'Sort 'a like a fungus,' Mort offered.

'If you say so. Hear anything from Parker Brothers about your board game?'

'Just a letter from a lawyer tellin' me they're lookin' at it.'

'That's encouraging,' I said.

'Maybe I ought to get *myself* a lawyer,' he said.

'I know a wonderful one here in New York. Jerry Winter. So, fill me in on your trip.'

'Pretty routine,' Morton responded. 'Seems like it's your trip ought to be talked about. I called the police headquarters where you were held, identified myself as a fellow law enforcement officer to some ugly fella, and told 'em to put you on. They said you were gone.

"Where?" I asked. He hung up on me. I'd like to get *his* name.'

'They're very busy at the precinct,' I said. I asked Seth whether he'd gone back to Nancy Morse's house after I'd left. He had, of course, being the dependable person that he is. But he saw nothing, no unidentified man.

'Thanks for trying,' I said. 'By the way, I'm no longer a material witness to Waldo's murder, nor a suspect in Susan Kale's death.'

'Good,' Seth said.

'I'm famished. Feel like a walk and a quick dinner?'

'Awful late,' Seth said, checking his watch, then patting his corpulent belly. 'But I am a mite hungry.'

We walked out onto Park Avenue and started uptown. It's a desolate part of town at night, lots of vehicular traffic but few pedestrians. We headed toward Fifth Avenue and its festive lights and decorations. As we waited at the corner of Fortieth and Madison, a homeless man stepped from a doorway and extended his hand to us. Mort spun around, grabbed the man's wrist, and announced, 'You're under arrest. I'm a police officer.'

'No, Morton, it's all right,' I said quickly. 'Here.' I handed the man a dollar bill. He thanked me, looked quizzically at Metzger, muttered 'weirdo,' and backed into the shadows of his doorway haven.

'Just a cold, homeless person,' I said.

'There's lots of them in the city.'

'Could have arrested him for vagrancy,' Morton said.

When I'd reached into my coat pocket for the dollar, I'd also pulled out the paper on which I'd jotted down that day's telephone messages. 'Excuse me,' I said, stepping into a public phone booth.

'*New York Post*,' an operator said.

'Editorial department please,' I said. 'Mr Bobby Johnson.'

CHAPTER FIFTEEN

Before leaving the hotel Sunday morning to meet with Bobby Johnson, I talked with Ruth Lazzara about that afternoon's press conference. No, I didn't need a limousine to take me. I'd get there on my own, and on time. And no, I would not discuss Waldo Morse or Susan Kale. I was a writer of murder mystery books and intended to stick to that in any subsequent interviews. She was disappointed but agreed. She didn't have a choice.

Seth Hazlitt and Morton Metzger wanted to accompany me to my brunch with Johnson, but I stood firm. 'That's why we're here, Jessica,' Seth said. 'Keep you out 'a further trouble.'

'I assure you, Seth, there will be no more trouble for this lady. I intend to promote my

168

book and soak up the holidays. Period. I want you to do the same.' To their glum faces I added, 'Let's meet here at six. Enjoy the city. We'll find a really good restaurant for dinner. And speaking of trouble, I suggest you two avoid it.'

Johnson had chosen a restaurant called Ernies, claiming it offered the best Sunday brunch in Manhattan. 'An "in" place,' he'd said. 'And my treat,' he added as additional inducement to join him. He didn't know that I didn't need extra inducements. I'd decided while sitting in a Manhattan jail cell that the best way to get out from the middle of murders in Manhattan—but still see the web of mystery surrounding Waldo and Susan Kale resolved— was to lay everything I knew on him. He could take it from there. After all, he was an investigative reporter, and a good one from what I'd observed. Time for me to play the bystander, feed him what information I had, and watch things develop.

I arrived at Ernies early, confirmed the reservation he'd made under his name, and waited outside rather than taking the table. The air was crisp and smelled clean. Well, relatively clean. I closed my eyes and imagined I was standing on the Maine coast inhaling its invigorating ocean breezes. I was deep into my reverie and didn't see or hear Johnson. 'Mrs Fletcher,' he said. 'Are you okay?'

My eyes snapped open. 'Oh, yes, of course. I

was daydreaming.'

'Didn't mean to startle you.'

'That's all right. I confirmed your reservation. Shall we go in?'

After being seated at a corner table, I got right down to business. 'The reason I agreed to meet with you, Bobby, is that I've decided to share with you what I know about Waldo Morse's murder, and the murder of Susan Kale.'

He smiled. 'Why the turnaround, Mrs Fletcher. Until now, you've treated me like the enemy. I want to be your friend.'

'In return for exclusive juicy stories,' I said.

'Sure. No such thing as a free brunch. But that doesn't mean we can't be friendly.'

I observed him across the table. He was a nice-looking young man, but someone who, no matter how hard he tried, would always appear slightly unkempt. He was losing his hair prematurely; an attempt to grow a beard was hampered by a lack of natural facial hair. It grew in sparse clumps. He looked perpetually tired, and I wondered about his lifestyle. Probably a night person. Did he have a special girl in his life? Maybe there wasn't time for that. So many questions fueled by my inherent curiosity. I didn't ask them, however. As much as I wanted to cooperate with him, I wasn't seeking friendship. Besides, my motives in meeting with him were as devious as his. I wanted him to get to the bottom of the murders for my sake, my self-interest. He was right. No such thing as a free brunch, no matter who paid the bill.

A pretty young waitress gave a theatrical presentation of the day's specials. An out-of-work actress, I judged, waiting tables to pay the rent until the big break came along. She wrote down our orders—eggs Benedict and a Bloody Shame for me (the British term for a Virgin Mary), and *huevos rancheros*, a Mexican egg dish, and the real thing, a Bloody Mary for Johnson—and started to walk away. She turned, narrowed her eyes at me, and said, 'You're a famous actress, aren't you? Your name is on the tip of my tongue.'

'Afraid not,' I said lightly. 'But I'm sure you'll be famous one day.'

She beamed, said, 'That's my goal.' She handed me a business card. 'If you hear of anything,' she said.

'Of course.' That was one of the appealing things about New York. Everyone walking around with big dreams and willing to sacrifice to realize them.

'Well,' Johnson said. 'Here we are. What's new in the life of Jessica Fletcher?'

'Quite a bit, Bobby. I visited Waldo Morse's wife, Nancy, in Cabot Cove yesterday. She told me some things I thought you'd be interested in.'

'You went home yesterday?'

'Yes, but only for a few hours.' I told him of

my furtive escape from Manhattan and of my unexpected, premature return. He found it amusing, which, in retrospect and from an observer's perspective, it probably was.

'I knew Waldo Morse from Cabot Cove.'

His eyebrows went up.

I told him everything I knew about Waldo, including his disappearance into the witness protection program.

'You say you talked to his wife.'

'Yes. She was in the process of moving.' I filled him in on Joe Charles and his relationship to Waldo and to Susan Kale. I did not, however, mention the third member of the intriguing triangle I'd uncovered, Detective Alphonse Rizzi. I'd raise him with Johnson when, and if, I felt the time was right.

'Where did Morse's wife move?' he asked.

'I don't know.' I wished I did. And then I remembered the yellow pages I'd torn from the pad in her kitchen, and which were back in my hotel room. If she'd pressed down hard enough when writing on the top pages, the ones I'd removed might have indentations that could be read using the old run-a-pencil-across-it technique. That was my intention when taking them, but I'd forgotten about it in the lunacy of the past two days.

Johnson had been taking notes on a small pad as I talked. He put it aside when our food was served, and we talked of things other than murder. When coffee arrived, he leaned across the small table and asked, 'Do you realize what we have here, Mrs Fletcher?'

'Please, call me Jessica. And no, I don't know what we have here. That's what I'm hoping you can provide.'

'We have the makings of a best-selling true-crime book.'

I sat back. '*We? True crime book? I'm not interested in that.'*

'Suit yourself, Jessica. I can write it myself. But I think it's only fair for you to share in the spoils. Make a great movie, TV miniseries.'

'Thank you for thinking of me, Bobby, but no thank you.' Was I acting precipitously in sharing information with him? He was obviously a young man with ambition, like our actress-waitress. Could I truly trust him? I decided on the spot that now that I'd gone this far with him, I might as well.

We parted with the understanding that we would share our knowledge of the murders with each other, but that I would no longer be actively seeking information.

'Think about my idea for a book,' he said as we shook hands on the sidewalk.

'Sorry to disappoint, but I won't be giving it a second thought, even a first one. Feel free to pursue it on your own.'

'Fair enough, Jessica. Keep in touch.'

Later, at dinner with Seth and Morton at a steak house near the hotel—we chose it to satisfy Morton's refusal to avoid red meat in his daily diet: 'Real men eat meat,' he was fond of saying, to Seth's chagrin—I was pumped for what I'd learned from the crusading young reporter.

'Nothing,' I replied. 'I talked, he listened. I'm afraid the reporters at the press conference this afternoon didn't learn much from me. All they wanted to talk about was Waldo and Susan Kale's murder. And I refused to discuss those things. Ruth Lazzara, Vaughan's publicity director, wasn't happy either. But I feel good about my decision to stick to what I know: writing books. I feel incredibly relieved, a heavy burden off my back. Bobby Johnson will investigate murder, and we'll investigate the wonders of this city. By the way, what did you do today?'

My question prompted a spirited replay by both men of their sightseeing. They'd spent most of the afternoon in F.A.O. Schwarz, which had brought out the child in both of them. Their faces glowed as they described the toys, and the children who marveled at them.

'Not such a bad place after all,' I said.

'The store?'

'The city itself.'

'I wouldn't go that far,' Cabot Cove's sheriff replied.

He'd worn his tan uniform, Stetson hat, and badge everywhere since arriving, which drew considerable reactions from most people, including patrons of the steak house. 'Damn near got killed by a couple 'a crazy taxi drivers. They wouldn't get away with drivin' like that back home.'

'No, they wouldn't, not with Sheriff Morton Metzger in charge,' I agreed. 'Shall we? This lady is getting sleepy.'

Which I remedied by climbing into bed soon after getting back to my suite, Miss Hiss curled at my feet. I closed my eyes and allowed sleep to quickly and quietly consume me.

CHAPTER SIXTEEN

I slept soundly but not long enough. The jangling of the phone next to my bed sent Miss Hiss scurrying for cover, and jarred me to an unsteady sitting position against the headboard. I shook my head and tried to read the time from the digital clock radio. It couldn't be. Five-fifteen? Maybe I'd slept all day, and it was early evening.

'Hello,' I mumbled, thankful the incessant, grating ringing had ceased.

''Mornin, Jess. Seth here.'

'Seth, it's five-fifteen.'

'I know that, and I apologize for waking you. But I thought it was important.'

'You're up,' I said, knowing immediately it was a stupid thing to say. Of course he was up. He was talking to me.

175

'Couldn't sleep. Nothing but sirens and horns beeping and garbage trucks rattling cans right outside my window. At any rate, I've been watchin' TV—CNN—quite a service to have, TV news twenty-four hours every day.'

'Uh-huh.'

'Just heard a report that a Catholic priest was murdered early this morning in St. Patrick's Cathedral, of all places.'

'How terrible. It was on CNN already?'

'Nope. Got that on a local channel. Certainly is a terrible thing. Seems nobody's safe. No safe *place*.'

There was silence.

'Why was it necessary to wake me at five in the morning to tell me this?'

''Cause it got me to thinkin' about this Waldo Morse mess. Seems to me Waldo was killed right next to that church.'

'That's right. But how would you know that?'

'You told me the corner where Waldo got it. Mort and I stopped in the cathedral yesterday. Some imposing place. Anyway, seemed to me that it might be a useful coincidence.'

'Hmmm. Maybe.' My thoughts leaped back to the first day I'd seen Waldo. A priest had approached him, and I'd found it interesting that Waldo had handed the priest something rather than the other way around. 'Any other details on TV about the priest being murdered?' I asked.

'Nope. I suppose you might as well go back

176

to sleep. See you at nine for breakfast.'

I was now wide-awake and craving a cup of hot coffee. I'm basically a tea drinker, but there are times when only coffee will do. 'Go back to sleep?' I said, laughing. 'Out of the question. See you in the dining room at seven.'

I knew I wouldn't hold out until seven, so I ordered coffee and a muffin from room service and turned on the television. The priest's murder was reported the minute the screen came to life.

'. . . *And, in Manhattan, a priest was shot and killed on the steps of St. Patrick's Cathedral early this morning. The priest, whose identity is being withheld pending notification of relatives, was shot three times in the chest while leaving the cathedral. It is not clear why he was there at that hour or whether he was a member of the cathedral diocese. Robbery has been ruled out as a motive, say police.'*

After enjoying the coffee and muffin, I took a quick shower, tossed on my sweats, and rode the elevator down to the lobby. Evidently my steadfast refusal at the press conference to not speak about *real* murders had had its intended effect. There was no one from the media ready to pounce on me. I went to a small store that sold newspapers. I didn't expect the priest's murder to be in early editions but bought them all anyway, scanned the headlines, and continued my morning constitutional at a brisk pace. I enjoy the early mornings. So many possibilities lie ahead. People seem hopeful as they hurry to work, purpose written on their faces, urgency in their step. Maybe that's why I've always written early in the day, using afternoons and evening for reading, and catching up on correspondence and paperwork. I've never understood writers who write all night and sleep all day. But they wouldn't understand my schedule either. Different body clocks, circadian rhythms marching to different drummers.

After breakfast, Seth and Morton headed off for more sightseeing and shopping—remarkable, I thought, how quickly they'd adopted the Christmas spirit in dreaded New York City—and I stayed in my suite returning phone calls, including a postmortem by Ruth Lazzara on the Sunday press conference. She'd received a number of calls that morning from the press, including offers for me to appear on afternoon television talk shows. I'd watched a few of them back in Cabot Cove and, frankly, they didn't impress me. I asked Ruth, 'Why would they want me? I've never slept with anyone but my husband, never abused a child, and *never* would talk on television about those things if I had.'

'But these are national shows, Jessica, with huge and loyal followings. The book will race to the top of the best-seller charts the day after you appear.'

'Sorry, Ruth, but I simply won't subject

myself to that type of situation.'

Her deep, dark sigh said many things; I was grateful she didn't express them.

I called Bobby Johnson at the *Post* but didn't reach him. I wondered what he knew about the priest's murder that morning. Chances were it was pure coincidence. But I'd learned over many years of plotting crimes for my books, and solving them, that taking coincidences for granted could prove misleading, if not dangerous. My books may be fiction, but there's nothing fictitious in this world that hasn't actually happened to someone.

My first appointment that day was an eleven-o'clock book signing at Shakespeare and Company, a popular Manhattan bookstore. Seth and Morton insisted upon joining me, and we took a cab from the hotel. It had started to flurry; the TV weatherman predicted one-to-three inches that day, a mere dusting back home but obviously cause for major concern to New Yorkers. I wondered if the weather forecast would keep people from attending the signing. It didn't. A large crowd had already gathered on the second-floor landing of the store, and it was only ten-thirty.

To my chagrin, there were reporters and photographers in the crowd, and they were soon joined by a camera crew.

'Seems to me we should leave,' Seth whispered in my ear. 'They brought you here to sign books, not to put yourself in a fishbowl.'

'It's all right,' I replied. 'Let them take pictures. As long as I don't have to answer questions.'

I ignored the media and got down to signing books, which proved to be enjoyable. No doubt about it. I'd relaxed considerably since the madness of the previous week. I felt at peace with myself and the world. Contrary to popular belief, New Yorkers can be friendly and helpful. One 'fan' filled me in on the best Christmas window displays in the city and offered to take me on a personal tour. Another brought me a tin of homemade frozen lasagna: 'I heard you say on a talk show that you liked Italian food,' she said sweetly. Mort Metzger took the lasagne from me and said after the woman had left with her autographed book, 'I'll get rid of it, Jess. Never know what some cuckoo might slip in it.'

The signing was scheduled to last until one, but at twelve-thirty there was still a line that descended down the stairs and wrapped around the back of the store. I'd be there another hour. I stood for a seventh-inning stretch, felt a sneeze coming on, and pulled a tissue from my purse.

'Hope you're not getting a cold,' Seth said.

'I don't think so,' I said. 'Well, back to business.' I twisted my hand to relieve writer's cramp and resumed my place at the table. The next person in line slid a book in front of me. I asked without looking up, 'To whom should I sign it?'

'To Waldo.'

I began to write, stopped, and looked up. He was disguised—a shaggy blond wig, heavy growth of beard, dark glasses, and a ski hat pulled down low over his forehead—but I knew I was peering into Waldo Morse's face.

'Waldo!' I said too loud.

'I've got to talk to you, Mrs Fletcher. Two o'clock at the library's main branch. Fifth and Forty-second. The third-floor reading room.'

'Two? The last time you asked me to meet you at two terrible things started happening.'

His expression was quizzical. A small smile formed on his lips. 'Two-fifteen?'

'Yes. Two-fifteen.'

I finished signing his book and handed it back to him. He said nothing and hurried down the stairs.

CHAPTER SEVENTEEN

I've suffered shocks before but none with the impact of seeing Waldo Morse alive. How could it be? I'd witnessed his murder on Fifth Avenue. Or had I? It wasn't even worthy of a question. Obviously, and despite popular myth, there is more than one Santa Claus in the world.

As I continued to sign books, my mind raced

back to that fateful day. I'd taken too much for granted, had made assumptions based upon shaky evidence and unreasonable expectations. I'd *expected* Waldo to be there and never questioned whether it was, in fact, him who had fallen. I'd been unable to see him with any clarity. So many people had stood between us. And there was that beard that covered his face. I *assumed* it was Waldo but had been fooled, like a magic show audience having its attention diverted from what the magician's hands are actually doing.

'It's Cora,' the woman standing in front of me said.

I looked up. 'What?'

'I said my name was Cora. You wrote "Dear Waldo."'

I laughed nervously. 'Sorry. My mind wandered.' Ruth slid another book in front of me to sign correctly.

After a few more near autographing mishaps, Ruth asked how I was feeling.

'Not well, I'm afraid,' I said. 'I'm a little dizzy and weak. Could we cut this short without alienating too many people?'

'Let me see what I can do.' After a whispered meeting, the store manager announced to those still in line that I had to leave at one-thirty to honor another commitment. There were groans of protest. I felt predictably guilty, but not to the extent of changing my mind. I attacked my autographing

182

task with renewed vigor.

'I knew it,' Seth said when I told him I was feeling ill and wanted to return to the hotel for a nap. He's a physician after all, my doctor for years.

'Just need some rest,' I said. 'I'll be good as new.' We stopped at a pharmacy where he bought me an assortment of over-the-counter cold remedies, which I promised to take.

'I'll stay with you in your room,' he offered.

'No, please, Seth. I won't be very good company because I'll be asleep. I'll call you the minute I wake up.'

By the time I reached the suite, the theory that if you lie, the lie will come true, gained credence. I *did* feel dizzy and weak. But I rationalized that it was the result of the confusion that swirled in my brain like leaves trapped in a corner on a windy day. What was going on here?

I meet Waldo Morse wearing a Santa costume on Fifth Avenue. He tells me to come back the next day at two. I return, only to see him gunned down in cold blood. But it isn't him. Someone else is killed. The police, particularly a detective named Alphonse Rizzi, don't seem to care.

I befriend a young woman who knew Waldo, and offer her shelter. She's murdered, too.

I receive a strange message informing me that someone by the name of Joe Charles 'will know.' I find Joe Charles, who lies to me about

183

his telephone. Despite my bumbling attempts at disguise, I discover that Charles knows Detective Rizzi well enough to meet with him at a jazz club. Susan Kale is there, too, one night before she's murdered.

Joe Charles disappears.

Waldo's wife, Nancy, hurriedly packs up her lovely home in Cabot Cove and takes off for points unknown.

A priest is slaughtered on the steps of St. Patrick's Cathedral. I'd seen a priest take something from Waldo on Fifth Avenue.

And now this. Waldo Morse stands in line to have me sign his book, which means he's very much alive. No Santa costume this time, but a different approach to incognito.

And yet another scheduled rendezvous.

I knew one thing. This meeting would result in answers to the myriad questions twisting in my brain. I would find out what I needed to know.

The main reading room of the New York Public Library was spacious and majestic. I'd taken the stairs at a fast clip and had to catch my breath at the top. I surveyed the room for Waldo. At least he hadn't changed costumes again. He was seated at a table, his face obscured by a large book. Most tables were occupied by more than one person. Fortunately, Waldo was alone. I quietly sat next to him, clasped my hands on the table, and stared straight ahead. His acknowledgment of

184

my arrival was a guttural grunt.

Without turning my head, I said quietly, 'I don't understand.'

Another grunt; he continued to pretend to read.

'To say I am in shock is a major understatement, Waldo.'

He turned his head slightly in my direction and shifted his eyes to take in surrounding tables, a hungry dog assuring that no other animal was about to take its food. His eyes locked on mine. 'I'm sorry you had to get involved in this, Mrs Fletcher. But I didn't ask you to recognize me. I didn't ask you to come up to me on Fifth Avenue.'

'Of course you didn't. Frankly, I'm sorry I did. But now that I have—now that I am involved—there are questions I would like very much to have answered.'

'Go ahead. I'll answer what I can.'

'Let's start with the obvious. You and I are sitting here together in the public library. But I saw you shot. Murdered.'

'It wasn't me.'

'I've concluded that. Who was it?'

'George Marsh.'

'Marsh,' I muttered. The name I'd heard at police headquarters. I said, 'I assumed that was a name you were using. I thought maybe you carried that name on a piece of identification because—well, because you're in the witness protection program.'

'Not anymore I'm not. Marsh wasn't a phony name I used. It belonged to a friend of mine who was out of work, broke and desperate.'

I sat back and looked up at the ornate ceiling. 'Why would someone shoot such a person?'

He said flatly, 'They thought it was me.'

He saw the confusion on my face—it was hard to miss—and so he leaned close. 'When you came up to me on the street, Mrs Fletcher, I panicked. I said I'd meet you the next day just to get rid of you. I went home that night and decided it was time to get away for a while. It isn't healthy in my line of work to be recognized. While I was deciding what to do, George Marsh stopped by. He looked like hell. He hadn't eaten in days and said he was ready to pack it in.'

'Commit suicide?'

'Yeah. So I came up with the idea of having George stand in for me for a couple of days. He and I were about the same height and weight. I figured that when you came back and found out it wasn't me, you'd just forget about it and I wouldn't have to worry about you. George agreed. I even told him to pocket the donations.'

'That's terrible,' I said.

'Not when you're hungry, Mrs Fletcher. Anyway, I wasn't in the mood for a debate on morality. I gave Marsh my Santa suit and split.'

I felt a sudden pang of anger. I'd been

186

defrauded in being led to believe that Waldo had been the one killed that day. 'And I thought it was you,' I said, unable to filter exasperation from my voice. 'Do you know what pain this has caused me, Waldo?'

'Sure. Sorry about that. But don't feel stupid thinking it was me. Like they say, everybody in a Santa suit looks the same.' His laugh was rueful.

I drew a deep breath. 'All right,' I said, 'this George Marsh person was shot because the killer thought he was you. Why?'

'Why what?'

'Why did someone want to kill *you*?'

'Sure you want to know?' Waldo asked, his eyes narrowing.

'I assume it's because of what happened to you back in Maine,' I said. 'The drug charge, the trial.'

'You got it, Mrs Fletcher. That episode turned my life around. I've been on the run ever since.'

'The drug dealers you testified against tried to kill you?'

'Maybe.'

'If not them, who?'

'I'm not sure. I have my ideas.'

'Waldo, I saw Nancy recently. Last Saturday as a matter of fact. I went to her house to inform her of your death, and to ask if she had any idea who might have wanted to kill you.'

'You did?'

187

'Yes. I didn't get there any too soon. Moving men were emptying the house.'

Until this moment, his expression and voice had been passive. But when I told him about Nancy's move, his face sagged as though a blast of hot air had hit a wax mask. 'Moving?' he said in disbelief. 'Where was she going?'

'I don't know. She wouldn't tell me.'

I could feel his body tense. He looked around the cavernous room, a cornered person seeking an escape route.

'I'm sorry to have to upset you with this news, Waldo.'

'They won't hesitate to kill her, Mrs Fletcher. They'll kill her and the kids if it suits their purpose.'

His frightened look now turned to sadness. His lips quivered. What a terrible life to be leading, I thought. I felt profoundly sad for him at that moment, and for Nancy and the children who'd suffered, too, as a result of his foolishness years ago. In retrospect, he probably would have been better off standing trial and paying for his crime. At least when it was over, he'd be free to pursue a normal existence, hopefully with Nancy and the kids. But the deal he'd cut with authorities had condemned him to a life of fear and suspicion, shadows and darkness.

He remained in his pensive mood a moment more, then turned and said, as though reading my thoughts, 'Mrs Fletcher, I made a stupid mistake years ago getting involved with drug dealers. I was young and trying to build a fishing business. It was hard, real hard. The money just wasn't there, and there was Nancy and the kids to support. I didn't intend to run drugs for long, just enough to build a stake. I couldn't make payments on the boat I'd bought, and the bank was threatening to repossess it.'

Which was no excuse for what you did, I thought. But I said only, 'Yes. It must have been difficult.'

He continued his introspective monologue. 'I've been trying to make it up to them—hell, to me—ever since. When I accepted the Feds' deal, I did it for my family. But they lied to me. They told me that if I testified and went into the witness protection program, I'd be settled in some pretty, quiet place where Nancy and the kids would eventually join me. Nobody would know where we were. The money wasn't great but we probably could have lived on it.' He chewed his cheek, his hands became fists on the table. 'I talked to Nancy about it, and she agreed it was the best thing to do. All we cared about was getting back together.'

'But they didn't live up to their promises?'

He slowly shook his head. 'No, they didn't. They kept pressuring me to testify against others.'

'There were other drug dealers you knew about?'

'No. They wanted me to infiltrate other drug rings. I refused. Then they got tough and reneged on some of the things they promised me and Nancy. That's when I told them to take their witness protection program and shove it.' He checked to see whether I was offended. I wasn't. He continued. 'I was out in Colorado when I decided to get out. I came to New York and got involved with the cops here as an informant, making friends with guys they wanted a line on and reporting back to them. I'll tell you this, Mrs Fletcher. It may not have been honorable, but the money sure was good. It meant Nancy and the kids could live nice. I sent them plenty. I didn't like snitching on people I'd gotten to know, but I did it.'

That Detective Alphonse Rizzi was a narcotics detective crossed my mind. I asked, 'Was Detective Rizzi your police contact?'

'Control,' Waldo corrected. 'He's been my control ever since I got involved. I was working for him the day you spotted me on Fifth.'

My eyebrows went up. No wonder Rizzi was so quick to arrive on the scene. He must have been close by observing Waldo. 'You were working for the police but pretending to collect charitable contributions as Santa Claus?' I asked, incredulous.

'I sure was, Mrs Fletcher. The cops were investigating drug dealing going on at St. Pats. They put me there because it gave me a good view of the action.'

190

Drugs in St. Patrick's Cathedral? The contemplation was shocking. Could it possibly be true? Was the priest I saw receiving something from Waldo a drug dealer? And there was the shocking story that very morning about a priest being shot at the cathedral.

Again, Waldo seemed to read my thoughts. 'Mrs Fletcher, the church—the cathedral—isn't involved in drug dealing. But a group in the city decided it was a perfect cover, wearing priests' garb and doing their dealing in and around the church.'

'I saw a priest approach the first day I saw you. Was he a priest, or a drug dealer?'

'An undercover cop.'

Of course, I thought. How silly of me not to know.

'Waldo, you know about Susan Kale.'

'Sure I do. That's one of the reasons I decided to make contact with you. I read about how you found her and all.'

'She was living with Joe Charles. Did you know that?'

'Yup. That was her mistake.'

'Mistake?'

'I'd call it a mistake. It got her killed.'

'Whoa, wait a minute,' I said. 'Are you saying that Joe Charles killed her?'

'I wouldn't be surprised.'

'Why? I mean, how do you know?'

'That's too long a story for now. I've already been in one place too long.'

'But surely—'

He cut me off by placing his hand on my arm and leaning closer, his eyes blazing with purpose. 'Mrs Fletcher, what you told me about Nancy moving is really upsetting. I have to find out where she is.'

'Do you think her life is in danger?' I thought of the male voice at her house, and my feeling that it was Joe Charles.

'Yeah, I do. Will you help me find them?'

I hesitated. But then the feelings of compassion I'd experienced earlier returned. 'I don't know what I can do, Waldo, but yes, I will try to help you find Nancy. You don't have any idea where she might have gone?'

He said in a whisper, 'Joe Charles. He'll know.'

My eyes opened wide. 'It was you who left that message.'

'Yeah.'

'Why? Why bother telling me about Joe Charles?'

'Once George was killed, and I knew it was me they intended to hit, I figured I wanted somebody else to be involved. If somebody else knew what was going down, it might take the pressure off. Sorry it was you I called, but I know your reputation for snooping into murders.'

'I'm not sure I'm pleased with that reputation. Why didn't you just call and identify yourself to me? Why did you feel it was necessary to have me continue to believe you were dead, that it was you who was shot instead of this Marsh fellow?'

'Because it was better for certain people to think I was dead.'

'Joe Charles?'

'Among others.'

'Susan Kale?'

'Sure.'

'But—but Detective Rizzi must have learned rather quickly that it wasn't you in the Santa suit.'

'That's right. He's one of the people I'd just as soon not see for a while. He won't be happy that I split, that's for sure.'

He suddenly jerked his head away, sat up tall, and looked out over the vast expanse of reading room. It was as though someone had flipped a switch that activated his antenna, set his nerve ends on alert status. 'I have to go,' he mumbled.

This time, I placed *my* hand on *his* arm. 'Please, Waldo, don't bolt on me. You've chosen to bring me into this. You ask my help in finding Nancy, yet continue to deal with me in bits and pieces, in bursts of revelation.'

He stood.

'Waldo. Sit down and listen to me,' I said sternly.

He sat, but it was obvious there wouldn't be any further meaningful conversation. He opened the large book he'd been perusing when I arrived and tore off a corner of a page. I winced. He pulled out a pen and scribbled the name of a restaurant, followed by the words Sea Cliff. He handed me the scrap. 'It's a little town on Long Island. I have a friend there. I think I'll hole up there a few days, probably through Christmas.'

Christmas! Today was Monday. Christmas was two days away.

'What do you want me to do?' I asked.

'If you want to continue this conversation, Mrs Fletcher, come out there tomorrow for lunch. I'll feel more comfortable there.'

I started to protest. My schedule was full through Christmas. More book signings. Interviews. A Christmas Eve party at the Buckleys'. And, of course, spending time with my Cabot Cove friends, Seth and Morton.

'Waldo, I really can't leave the city. Why not continue the conversation right here? No one knows I'm here. I certainly didn't tell anyone. In fact, I lied about where I was going this afternoon.'

His response was, 'I'll be at Gallagher's at noon tomorrow.'

I watched him disappear down the stairs, sat back, and sighed, staring at the tabletop. My good intentions of removing myself from Waldo's twisted life now seemed distant and feeble. I looked around the reading room. I've never considered myself a paranoid person but at that moment, every person, every thing looked suspicious, posed a threat. Waldo had rubbed off on me. That cold realization prompted me to leave the library and to slowly wander back to the hotel, the holiday street scenes and festive windows obscured by the black, murky thoughts that enveloped me.

CHAPTER EIGHTEEN

By the time I completed the short walk back to the hotel, my somber mood had been replaced by fiery determination. Things had gone far enough—the furtive meetings, the disguises (including my own comical getup), people supposedly dead and then showing up alive, the shadowy world of the witness protection program and everything else that intruded upon what was supposed to have been a pleasant bit of book promoting, and deck the halls with boughs of holly in New York City.

The minute I got to my suite, I called the room shared by Seth and Morton. Morton answered. He sounded groggy. He had obviously been taking a nap, although he would never admit that. He was one of those people who considered midday naps to be, at best, a sign of weakness and sloth.

'Wake you?' I asked pleasantly.

'No. It's the middle of the day.'

'Yes. Well, Mort, I want you to do me a big

195

favor.'

'Anything you say, Jess.'

'Did you notice the name of the moving company that was at Nancy Morse's house the day we were there?'

'Can't say that I did,' he replied. 'But I did take note it was from Portland.'

'Splendid. Would you be a dear and call every moving company in Portland?'

'Might be quite a few, Jess.'

'I know, but this is important. Even urgent. I seem to remember seeing North American Van Lines on the truck. It must be a Portland mover licensed to represent that national company.'

'That'd narrow it down some,' he said.

'Use your law enforcement credentials to find out where the movers took Nancy. And by the way, Mort, don't worry about long-distance charges on your room bill. Buckley House will pay for it.'

I was about to make the second call on my mental list when the phone rang. 'Jessica Fletcher?' The operator had a distinctly British accent. I confirmed. 'Please hold for Inspector Sutherland.' Moments later, a delightful Scottish brogue said, 'Jessica, George Sutherland here.'

'How wonderful to hear your voice, George. What time is it in London?'

'Bedtime.'

'How in the world did you find me? I mean, I'm in New York publicizing my latest book—

things distinctly not literary have been happening—'

He laughed knowingly. 'So I've been reading. From what I gather, you're up to your neck in nasty business again. Murder, they say.'

'Make that plural. I could use a distinguished Scotland Yard inspector at my side to help sort things out. But how did you—?'

'Find you? Elementary, my dear Jessica. You told me that whenever you visit New York you stay at this Sheraton-Park Avenue Hotel. A jewel in Manhattan, you said.'

'You have a good memory. Actually, I started out staying with my publisher and his wife but moved here when the fur started to fly, as the saying goes.'

'Wish I could accommodate you, Jessica. Being at your side. But that's out of the question.' I hurriedly indicated that I was engaging only in wishful thinking. He said, 'I'm leaving first thing in the morning for home. The holidays and all.'

Home for George Sutherland was a tiny village at the northernmost tip of Scotland, a town called Wick. He'd been born there and, as he explained when we first met in London, his family had left him a castle of sorts overlooking a body of water called Pentland Firth. 'Barren and desolate,' he'd told me over tea at Brown's Hotel, but equally beautiful and inspiring. 'Time Jessica Fletcher planned a visit to Wick,' he'd written on a few occasions. The temptation was great, the time impossible to find. But one day . . .

'Can I be of any long-distance help?' he asked.

'Not unless you know something about our witness protection program.'

'Afraid I can't help you there. Oh, now, wait a sec. Let me back up a minute. I met a chap when attending your FBI's international conference on criminal investigative techniques. As I recall, his area of expertise was that witness program. Want his name?'

'Please.' I wrote 'William Tomic' on a pad. George even had his direct dial number in Washington.

I thanked him for the information.

'When are you visiting us again, Jessica?'

'Just as soon as my schedule permits.'

'Much too vague. We Scots have a saying. *Don't gie me the gunk*.'

'Translation needed.'

'Don't disappoint me, Jessica. *I be keen o*.'

I smiled. 'Yes, I'm fond of you, too.' My eyes became moist. 'It was sweet of you to call, George. Have a splendid Christmas at home. We'll keep in touch.'

'That we will. And you be careful. Sounds to me like you're dealing with loutish people. Merry Christmas.'

I called William Tomic in Washington. After being shunted between operators, he came on the line. 'What a pleasure receiving a call from Jessica Fletcher,' he said. 'I've read all your books. At least I think I have.'

'Including the new one?' I asked.

'Not yet. But now that you've called, I'll hightail it to my nearest bookstore.'

'No need,' I said. 'I'll be happy to send you one.'

'Autographed?'

'Of course.'

With that bit of business out of the way, I told him I was doing research for my next work and needed to know a little about how the Federal Witness Protection Program worked.

'Shoot,' he said.

'Is it possible for someone in that program to decide to leave it?'

'Sure, but only if the person is crazy enough to surface after having turned state's evidence. Not an especially healthy thing to do.'

'I would imagine,' I said. 'I'm creating a plot in which someone in the program decides to leave, and then becomes an informant for local police. Is that reasonable?'

He paused. 'Yes. I've personally known a few who've done that.'

'Why would anyone do that?' I asked.

'A couple of reasons. Tired of the clandestine life and wanting to get back into the mainstream. Family considerations. But mostly, money is the motivator.'

'Uh-huh. When someone goes into the

witness protection program, is he paid enough to live well, to support a family?'

'No. Well, I suppose it depends upon your definition of "living well." Nobody gets rich in the program, that's for certain.'

'But could a person get rich by coming out of the program and turning informant for some law enforcement agency, say the New York City police?' I realized the minute I asked the question that I'd tipped my hand. Tomic's change of tone confirmed it.

'You know, Mrs Fletcher, I've been following your escapades since your arrival in New York. Are you sure you're researching a book, or trying to get some answers to the murders you've witnessed?'

I had to smile. He didn't miss much. 'Let's just say a little of both,' I said.

'Okay. A little of both. To answer your question. Yes, a good informant can make a lot more money than what the Federal Government pays in the program. I've known snitches who've become millionaires. Of course, that depends upon the quality of the information they provide.'

'I see. I don't have any other questions at the moment, but I would appreciate being able to get back to you.'

'Any time, Mrs Fletcher.' I took down mailing information to send the book, thanked him again, and hung up.

I was glad I'd made the call. Obviously,

200

Waldo was being straight with me, at least concerning having left the program and becoming an undercover informant for the New York City police. That was comforting considering all the lies (disinformation is the politically correct term these days) I'd received since this whole affair started.

The phone rang again. It was the hotel operator informing me that Ms Lazzara was on her way up to the suite. I was scheduled to be interviewed in twenty minutes by a writer doing an article for *Parade*. I quickly herded Miss Hiss into the bathroom, gave her a fresh supply of food and water, closed the door, and awaited Ruth's arrival.

She was in her usual state of high anxiety, talking fast, hands fluttering like birds in search of a perch. '*Parade* wants to focus on the Marjorie Ainsworth murder you were involved with in London. Why, I don't know, but that's what the writer wants, so we'd better give it to her.'

'Goodness,' I said, 'I'd better spend a few minutes remembering the details of that.'

'Talk in generalities,' Ruth said, fluffing pillows on the couch. 'By the way, Oprah still wants you, and I think I can get Donohue to go with it. Sure you won't change your mind?'

I sighed. She certainly was tenacious. 'No, I really would prefer not to.'

'Suit yourself.' As she started to straighten magazines on a glass table next to the couch, I noticed she was poised to toss scraps of paper on which I'd made notes into a basket. 'Oh, no,' I said, taking them from her. Included were pages from the yellow legal pad I'd confiscated from Nancy Morse's house in Cabot Cove. 'You don't happen to have a pencil, do you?' I asked.

She quickly pulled a ballpoint pen from her purse.

'No, I need a pencil. An old-fashioned number two lead pencil.'

'Can't help you.'

The phone rang; the writer from *Parade* had arrived. I put the papers in my purse, placed it in my bedroom closet, and returned to the living room as Ruth opened the door for the writer, Carolyn Dobkin, an older woman wearing a gray suit as severely cut as her gray hair. The interview, which took an hour, was pleasant and went smoothly. But answering questions about the murder of the world's greatest mystery writer, Marjorie Ainsworth, whom I was privileged to have befriended and in whose English manor house I was unfortunate to have been a guest the night she was murdered, was both pleasurable and painful. It turned out Ms Dobkin had written a book analyzing Ainsworth's writings. Small wonder she wanted to focus upon that.

After Dobkin had left, Ruth went over my schedule for that evening and the following day. I was to be a guest at an agent-author cocktail party at the Mercantile Library hosted by the New York chapter of the Mystery Writers of America. Immediately following that was another party for Buckley House's sales force, which, Vaughan had impressed upon me, was perhaps the most useful group I would meet while in New York. And then there was dinner—another dinner—this one with the head of a German publishing conglomerate that had recently purchased a major stake in Buckley House.

The following day, Christmas Eve, was no less hectic. A morning book signing, lunch with the head buyer from Barnes & Noble, a couple of interviews in the afternoon, and then Christmas Eve with the Buckleys at their Dakota apartment.

'You'll have to cancel the lunch,' I said.

'I can't do that, Jessica.'

'Sorry, but if I don't spend a couple of hours finishing up Christmas shopping, I'm going to have some very disappointed people back home. As it is, I can't get the gifts to them in time for Christmas, but at least I can call with conviction to tell them presents are on their way. Please, I've been cooperative, I think. Do me this favor.'

Ruth exhibited a rare smile, nodded, put her hand on my shoulder, and said, 'Of course. I've dealt with a lot of authors. You are undoubtedly the best I've ever worked with. Do your shopping.'

Her words warmed me. Of course, I wasn't being truthful about my reason for canceling the luncheon. I'd decided to head for the small town on Long Island to meet Waldo Morse. Call it throwing good money after bad. Call it an obsession. Call it what you will. He'd asked for my help in finding Nancy and the children. If anything happened to them and I hadn't expended every effort, I'd have trouble living with myself.

'Ready for the mystery writers' party?' Ruth asked.

'I will be in a few minutes. I brought a special red dress with me to wear over the holidays. I think it would be perfect for tonight, provided it still fits after all these meals you've insisted I eat. Give me ten minutes.'

I rejoined her in the living room wearing the dress which, strangely, seemed to have shrunk an inch.

'You look lovely,' Ruth said. 'Come on, time to head out.'

I was closing the door behind me when I heard the phone ring. We looked at each other. 'Should I?' I asked.

She shook her head. 'They'll take a message. We're running late.'

I decided on the ride down in the elevator to stop at the desk to see who the most recent caller had been. But by the time we reached the lobby, I'd forgotten about it. Had I stopped, I would have been handed this message written by the operator:

Nancy Morse called.
Urgent she speak with you.
Will call again.
Left no number.

CHAPTER NINETEEN

'I'd never been so disappointed in my life,' said one of the hundreds of guests at the Mystery Writers of America's cocktail party. 'Marjorie had promised to personally accept her Edgar Award. It was the best-attended awards dinner we'd ever had. And then she sent that telegram at absolutely the final, last minute expressing her regrets. Did she ever tell you, Jessica, the *real* reason she didn't attend? I mean, after all, you were so close to her.'

'No. I don't recall her saying anything about it,' I replied.

I'd been on the receiving end of countless questions about Marjorie Ainsworth, the acknowledged grande dame of the murder mystery genre unless, of course, you belonged to the Agatha Christie school.

'At least Agatha shared herself with her public,' said one of those.

I was surrounded by a dozen people, most of them authors, a few agents. Discerning the difference didn't depend upon the different-colored badges they wore. The variation in dress was sufficient. The agents tended to wear business suits. The writers dressed like—well, like writers.

'Marjorie was a quintessential recluse,' I said, slightly annoyed that I'd been put in the position of having to defend my dear departed friend. 'Excuse me,' I said.

My agent, Russ Checkett, had just arrived. I was delighted, relieved, and somewhat surprised to see him. He'd returned that afternoon from an extended stay in Czechoslovakia where he'd conferred with his newest client, a Nobel Prize-winning novelist. The fatigue on his face testified to his lack of sleep. 'Russ,' I said above the drone of party blatherskite.

He gave me a hug and a kiss on the cheek. 'Holding up?' he asked.

'Better than you, I would say. You look exhausted.'

'Getting a little too old for this kind of frenetic globe-trotting,' he said. 'Buy you a drink?'

'A little white wine.'

He returned from the bar with my wine and a large, amber Black Label on-the-rocks for himself.

'Frankly, you've arrived in the nick of time,' I said. 'Like the cavalry. If people aren't asking me about Marjorie Ainsworth, they all seem to have ideas for a locked-room mystery to out-Poe Poe.'

Russ laughed and clinked his glass against mine. 'I've been out of touch, but the office has kept me up-to-speed about what's been going on with you. My secretary says you've single-handedly boosted the Manhattan murder rate above the national average.'

'I wish you wouldn't put it that way,' I said. 'But yes, it has been an interesting visit. Vaughan and his people are delighted, I suppose, at the publicity. I could do without it.'

'Could we grab a couple of quiet minutes?' Russ asked. 'I need to talk to you, but don't know how long I'll last.'

'You're a real trouper, Russ, to be here after being on an airplane all night.'

'All part of the service to my favorite author.' He led me by the elbow to a relatively quiet corner of the room. 'So, tell me about this new book of yours,' he said.

My face reflected my puzzlement. 'What new book? I haven't started it yet. I don't even have a plot.'

His was a skeptical smile. 'As I understand it, the plot has already been written for you.'

'What are you saying to me?' I asked.

'That I think it's a wonderful idea for you to do a true-crime book based on your experiences in New York.'

'But I—'

'It could be a blockbuster, Jessica. The

world's most famous mystery writer turns to solving real crime. I love it.'

Bobby Johnson!

Russ confirmed it. 'My only concern is to what extent this Bobby Johnson from the *Post* can contribute to the work. It's your name that will sell the book. But we can't brush him off. After all, he did contact the office. And the proposal was pretty good.'

'Proposal?'

'Yes. Surely you've seen it. I was impressed with its thoroughness. He's a good writer.'

'And the proposal is for a book by Mr Johnson and me, sharing authorship?'

The pleasant glow on Russ's face turned serious. 'You aren't telling me that you haven't agreed to this with Johnson, are you?'

'That is exactly what I'm telling you.' I told him about my brunch with Johnson and his suggestion that we do such a book together. 'I turned him down flat,' I said.

'Well, that does put a different spin on things. But don't discount it out-of-hand, Jess. Could be a pleasant respite to be writing about something real. We have other novelist clients who occasionally turn to nonfiction to change pace. Let's talk more about it. Free tomorrow?'

'Tomorrow is Christmas Eve. I have some appearances to make. There's a party at Vaughan's house in the evening.'

'I know. I'll be there.'

'Splendid. Maybe we can continue this

conversation then.'

Russ stayed another twenty minutes, excused himself, and left.

'Jessica Fletcher, I must speak with you immediately,' said a wisp of a man with shoulder-length mouse-colored hair.

'I'm just about to leave,' I said. 'I have another engagement.'

'It will only take a moment. Please. It is very important.'

I internalized my sigh and leaned closer to better hear him. Not only was he short, he had lips that didn't move when he spoke. Lip-reading was out of the question. 'I've just finished reading your new book, and there is a serious error in it.'

I stifled a smile. Every book I've ever written elicited mail from 'experts' taking me to task for missing an important point of fact. I prefer to receive those objections by mail. Having to face my accuser proved more difficult.

'You have the victim dying within twenty-four hours of mushroom poisoning,' he said. 'That doesn't happen. It usually takes two or three days for *amanita phalloides* to destroy the liver.'

I replied, 'I appreciate your comment but I disagree. Yes, it often takes longer for poison mushrooms to kill the victim, but not always. My victim died of a collapse of his circulatory system. I checked it very carefully with a forensic pathologist, a friend at the University of Maine Medical Center.'

He wasn't deflated by my response. Instead, he puffed up to an inch taller and said through clenched teeth, 'I respect the credentials of this person you consulted, but I've studied the field of mushroom poisoning extensively, as well as other poisons. Every one of my books is totally accurate.'

'I don't doubt that at all,' I said, desperate to escape. 'I would enjoy reading one of your books.'

'I'll be happy to send you a manuscript.'

'Manuscript? Haven't they been published?'

He stood on tiptoe and said in a voice dripping with anger and frustration, 'The publishing industry is corrupt. No one is published without paying off editors. I will never stoop to that.'

I considered pointing out that I had never paid off anyone, but realized it was futile. Instead, I said, 'I think you're probably right about mushroom poisoning. I'll be more careful next time.' And I was gone, moving past him with the fluid skill of a premiere football running back.

I rounded up Ruth Lazzara and suggested we head for our next appointment, the cocktail party with Buckley House's sales force. She seemed happy to be rescued, too. Once word got around the party that she was head of publicity for Buckley House, she was inundated by fledgling authors seeking an in with the prestigious publisher. We retrieved our coats—not an easy task considering there was one young man trying to keep track of hundreds of garments—bid farewell to a few people, and headed down the stairs. We were halfway to the lobby when I spotted Bobby Johnson coming through the front door. 'Jessica,' he said loudly, wedging his way through knots of people. He reached the foot of the stairs. 'I have to talk to you,' he said.

'Yes, I certainly think you do.'

'We have to go,' Ruth said, pulling me by the arm. Johnson took my other arm. I felt like I was on a medieval torture rack. Eventually they pulled in the same direction and we ended up in a corner.

'Mrs Fletcher doesn't have time for interviews right now,' Ruth said.

'I don't want an interview,' Johnson replied. 'Please, just two minutes.'

'Would you excuse us, Ruth,' I said. When she was gone, I said to Johnson, 'How dare you approach my agent and suggest I'm interested in doing a book with you?'

I couldn't read whether his expression was contrite or smug. His tone, however, said he considered my upset to be unjustified. 'Mrs Fletcher—Jessica—you are some hard lady to track down these days.'

'And I intend to keep it that way. Why did you go to Russ Checkett with your fraudulent claim that we intend to work together?'

211

'Hey, calm down. I figured there was nothing to lose by contacting your agent. I didn't tell him you agreed. I just said we'd talked about it and that I thought it would make a best-seller.'

'You had no right.'

'Okay. I had no right. But hear me out. You'd like to know the whereabouts of this mysterious Joe Charles character. Am I right?'

'Yes. I would like to know where he is.' My matter-of-fact expression of interest hardly reflected how anxious I was to receive that information. If Waldo was right—that Joe Charles had been behind the attempt to murder him on Fifth Avenue—and if I was right that it had been Joe Charles at Nancy Morse's house the day I visited—finding Charles could be the key to Nancy's survival.

'Well?' I said.

A smirk crossed Bobby's face. 'Hey, Jessica, tit for tat as they say. If I tell you how to find Joe Charles, what do I get in return?'

There goes that free lunch again, I thought. I asked, 'What is it you want from me?'

'The go-ahead to your agent for us to do this book together.'

'Absolutely not.'

'Suit yourself,' Johnson said, shrugging. 'But finding Joe Charles might answer all your questions about why your buddy, Waldo Morse, got killed.'

Ruth frantically waved for me to join her. 'Where will you be later tonight?' I asked.

'At the paper until ten, ten-thirty. Then home. You have both numbers.'

'Yes, I do. I'll call you later.'

'I'll be waiting with bated breath,' he said.

As Ruth and I went to the street, I realized how dramatically my perception of Bobby Johnson had changed during those few minutes. When we'd first met, I disliked him and his groveling for a story. But then he put forth a different, less predatory face. Now, my feelings were what they'd been initially. He was not to be trusted.

It also occurred to me as we climbed into the waiting town car that he still thought Waldo Morse was dead. That information could prove to my advantage, depending upon how I chose to dispense it.

'Where are you?' Ruth asked.

I snapped back to the here and now of the back-seat. 'Just reeling from all the conversation,' I said. 'So many people writing books, so few opportunities for them to see their work published.'

'It's a tough business.'

The party for the sales force was held in the Wings Club, in what used to be the Pan Am Building on Park Avenue. How could there be an aviation industry without the airline that opened the world to travelers? I wondered as we rode the elevator. But nothing is forever, as they say, which I hoped would prove to be true where the party was concerned.

'Your book is breaking all sales records, Jessica,' the vice president of sales, Bill Kelly, told me.

'That's wonderful news,' I replied. 'You and your people have obviously been busy.'

'Can't sell a bad book,' he said. 'I'm looking forward to your next. Interesting idea turning to true crime.'

'What?'

'The true-crime book about the Santa Claus murder. Will that be the title? The Santa Claus Murder?'

'I don't think so. I mean—excuse me.'

The party didn't last long, for which I was grateful. No matter who I talked to, the subject of my 'new book' came up. The publishing gossip mill was evidently more potent than even Cabot Cove's.

We left the Wings Club with a larger contingent than when leaving the mystery writers' party. Vaughan and Olga Buckley, Bill Kelly and three Buckley House executives would also attend dinner with the German businessman, Wolfgang Wurtzman, who now controlled, to some extent, the publishing house's future fortunes. Our chauffeur-driven limousines were parked on a ramp at the side of the building. Olga and I stood on the sidewalk and chattered as the group decided who would ride in which car. I glanced beyond her to a walkway across the ramp. A man in a tan raincoat and dark knitted watch cap

214

observed us. I hadn't noticed him at first. Now that I had, he quickly turned and walked south in the direction of Park Avenue.

'Your dress is lovely,' Olga said.

My eyes remained on the man as he continued to distance himself. 'Thank you,' I said absently. He disappeared around a corner.

'Anything wrong?' Olga asked.

'No, just a little battle-weary. Sorry.'

The Buckleys and I would ride together. Olga got in, and Vaughan waited for me to do the same. I was about to when a car suddenly appeared from the direction in which the man in the watch cap had disappeared. It approached slowly—very slowly. I looked into the driver's window as it came abreast. I didn't recognize the driver, but I certainly knew the man in the front passenger seat. Detective Alphonse Rizzi. No question about it, not with his memorable profile. He looked directly at me, then snapped his head away.

'You'll love the view of Manhattan from the River Café, Jessica,' Olga said. 'It's Mr. Wurtzman's favorite restaurant when in New York.'

Another fancy restaurant held little appeal for me. I glanced through the rear windshield to see whether Rizzi's car was following, but it was impossible to tell with so much traffic. By the time we had crossed to the Brooklyn side of the East River, had been ushered to our window table, and I'd been introduced to

Wolfgang Wurtzman as 'the pillar of Buckley House,' I'd almost forgotten about having seen my detective friend again. But not completely. Seeing him had created a gnawing sense of apprehension that would stay with me the entire evening.

CHAPTER TWENTY

'. . . *Da klatscht keiner Beifall—das ist das Ungeziefer, das mit den Flugeln schlagt.*'

One of Buckley House's executives laughed heartily at the punch line of Mr Wurtzman's joke. The rest of the table, including me, also laughed but only because our host's delivery was so animated.

'Wolfgang told the actress that it wasn't applause she was hearing. It was insects flapping their wings,' the German-speaking member of our party explained. We laughed a little harder and louder this time, although it didn't strike me as especially funny. But I didn't want to be impolite.

I tried to dismiss having seen Detective Rizzi, and the call I was to make later that evening to Bobby Johnson. It wasn't easy, but focusing upon the view of Manhattan's twinkling lights, and the food—my appetizer of fresh oysters with a minignonette sauce, and an entree of perfectly prepared red snapper—

helped.

A great deal of wine was consumed by everyone at the table with the exception of Olga and me. Wurtzman, a gregarious, heavyset gentleman with round red cheeks, small green eyes, and thinning hair, became even more expansive as the long, thin bottles of *Trockenbeerenauslesen*, expensive German white wine, disappeared.

As we left our table and headed for the lobby, Wurtzman, who spoke perfect English when he wasn't telling jokes in German, said to me, 'Jessica Fletcher, you are one of the reasons I invested in Buckley House.'

'That's very flattering,' I said.

'I want you to know that every resource under my control will be available to help sell your books. Might I also say that not only are you one of the world's best writers, you are a beautiful and charming woman.'

I flushed a bit and thanked him for his kind words. *'Auf Wiedersehen,'* I added, coming up with the only German phrase I knew.

He took both my hands and said, 'Yes, until we meet again.'

We were about to leave the restaurant when a hostess grabbed my arm. 'Mrs Fletcher? You are Jessica Fletcher?

'Yes.'

'There's a telephone call for you.'

Who would be calling me at the River Café? I wondered. Probably Seth or Morton. The hostess handed me a phone at the desk. 'Hello?' I said.

'If you want a merry Christmas, Fletcher, butt out.' The man hung up.

I stayed at the desk a few moments to regain my composure before joining the others outside. Ruth Lazzara and I shared a car back to the Sheraton-Park Avenue. She offered to buy me a nightcap, but I declined, said good night, and entered the hotel. As I crossed the lobby and waited for the elevator, the warning voice on the phone at the restaurant repeated in my head like a tape loop playing it over and over. The elevator took what seemed to me to be an inordinate amount of time to arrive, and ascended slower than usual. I watched the light for each floor come and go: *If you want a merry Christmas, Fletcher, butt out.*

Miss Hiss greeted me by rubbing against my legs. I tossed my coat on a chair and went to pick up the phone to call Johnson. The message light was flashing. I'd call down for my messages later. I dialed his number at the *Post*, but was told he'd left for the evening.

I called his home number. He picked up on the first ring. 'I figured you wouldn't call,' he said.

'Why would you think that?' I asked. 'I'm sorry it's late. I was at dinner and—'

'Do you want to know where Joe Charles is?' He sounded angry.

'That's why I'm calling.'

218

'He's performing in a little joint tonight.'

That surprised me. If he was serious about disappearing, why would he make a public performance? Then again, I reasoned, he had to eat. And, of course, appearing in a tiny, off-the-beaten-track jazz club did not necessarily translate into a 'public performance.'

'Where?' I asked.

'Not so fast,' Johnson said. His voice still had a nasty edge. 'I'm not giving you this information out of the goodness of my heart, Jessica. I can run with this story on my own.'

'Then why don't you?' I asked.

'Because I think you and I could make one hell of a score by working together. But you have to back off on this attitude about not collaborating with me on a book.'

I was being blackmailed, and that made *me* angry. There was nothing that would cause me to work with him on a book. I'd made that clear, and my resolve had not changed.

But someone's life was at stake here, Nancy Morse, and possibly her children. If I summarily shut Johnson off, he would pursue the story without having a clue that her life was in jeopardy. Would that be sufficient motivation for him to cooperate with me without having to make a commitment to a book? He didn't seem like an especially sentimental person. Ambition was written all over his sleeve, and I've learned over the years that people driven to that extent by ambition seldom care whose body gets in the way. But it was worth a try. I said, 'Nancy Morse, Waldo's wife, is in danger, Bobby. That danger might come from Joe Charles. There's more at stake here than a story—or any book. Please, tell me where he is. If I can talk to him, it might save her life.'

I waited for him to digest what I'd said and to respond. Finally, he said, 'Are you being straight with me, Jessica?'

'Yes, I am.'

'Why would his wife be in danger? Joe Charles? The guy is just a musician.'

'Maybe, maybe not.' I'd debated during his silence whether to tell him that Waldo Morse was, in fact, alive. I decided to, and did.

'What? Santa Claus is alive?'

'Yes.'

'How do you know?'

'I spoke with him.'

'Jesus. I mean—what a story!'

'Where is Joe Charles appearing?'

'He's—'

'I won't ask again, Bobby, and I won't grovel. I assure you I will not commit to doing a book with you. You'll have to make your own moral judgement. If Nancy Morse ends up dead, it will rest on your conscience. Maybe you can write in your next story how you indirectly helped bring about the death of a woman—and her children.'

I knew I was being melodramatic but didn't

220

care. The negotiation had gone on long enough. Either he agreed, or he didn't. If he didn't, I was in a quandary because I would not learn how to contact Joe Charles. All I could do was hope that he would see things my way, if only to find out more about Waldo being alive.

'Okay,' he said. It brought a smile to my face. 'But don't do an end-run on me, Jessica. We'll go see him together. Remember, we're a team.'

I ignored his comment. 'Where will I meet you?'

'Come to my place.' He gave me his address, an apartment building on the Upper West Side.

'Can't we just meet where Joe Charles is appearing?'

'No. Come here. We can talk a little bit before going there.'

I didn't like having to go to his apartment, nor did I see the need for any further talks between us. But he held the cards, as they say. Unless I chose to toss in my hand, I had to go with what I'd been dealt. I told him I'd be there as quickly as I could.

I threw on my coat, took a fast peek into the bathroom to make sure Miss Hiss had water, and raced from the suite, rode the elevator down, heart pounding, quickly crossed the lobby and got into a cab. I gave the driver Johnson's address and sat back, my mind functioning at a gallop. Had things happened at a more leisurely pace, I might not be in the cab,

221

might not be going to an apartment somewhere in Manhattan and then to an unnamed jazz club in search of a musician who possibly was a murderer.

But things hadn't happened slowly. They'd taken on their own pace and urgency, and I was swept up in the current, feeling very much like an unfortunate insect in a swimming pool about to be sucked into the skimmer.

CHAPTER TWENTY-ONE

Every taxi driver I'd had since arriving in New York drove as though he (in one case a she) was competing in the Indy 500. But now that I wanted to get to my destination as quickly as possible, I ended up with a driver who, when it came time to sell his vehicle, wanted to claim it had been driven by a little old lady from Pasadena. But we eventually reached Bobby Johnson's apartment building, a decaying structure I assumed had once been a magnificent home. It was located in the low hundreds, a few doors from Riverside Drive. What a magnificent neighborhood this must have once been. I paid the driver and thanked him for a sane ride.

He smiled. 'Life's too short to get yourself killed,' he said.

How right you are, I thought as I

approached the steps leading up to the front door. Unlike the building in which Joe Charles lived, this door was secured, and buzzers to apartments were connected. I found Johnson's nameplate and pushed the button. A sharp buzz was returned. I pushed open the door and stepped into the foyer. Another door gave me access to the first-floor hallway. A small elevator was to my right and waiting. I pushed Six. When I stepped out on to the sixth floor, Bobby stood in his open doorway. 'Hi,' he said.

'Hi,' I said.

'Come on in.'

I'd expected the worst. Why, I don't know. The address, I suppose, and a preconceived notion of the sort of lifestyle he led. But there I was assuming things again, as I'd done that day on Fifth Avenue when I *assumed* it was Waldo Morse who'd been shot.

The apartment was spacious, nicely decorated and spotlessly clean. I was immediately drawn to a room at one end that overlooked the Hudson River. 'What a beautiful view,' I said.

'Better than looking out on to somebody's air shaft.'

I surveyed the rest of the apartment. Its only disconcerting aspect was its dim lighting. A few small lamps cast ominous shadows as their low-wattage light fell on objects in the living room. Samuel Barbour's *Adagio for Strings*, one of the most somber pieces of music ever written and played at virtually every state funeral, came from unseen speakers, adding to the room's funereal atmosphere.

'Well, are we ready to go?' I asked, injecting cheer into my voice.

'In a few minutes,' Johnson said. He went through a doorway to another room. I wondered what I was supposed to do next. When he didn't return, I followed to where he'd gone. It was his office, or study. He sat behind a small desk. The light from a single desk lamp was the room's only illumination aside from the eerie glow from a color computer monitor. He looked up at me and said, 'Come here, Jessica. Sit down. I want to discuss something with you.'

I continued to stand in the doorway. 'What is it you want to discuss?' I asked.

'This.' He pressed a few keys on his keyboard, and a dot matrix printer went into action. When it had completed its task, Bobby tore off the document it had printed, carefully removed the perforations from the edges, and laid it on the desk. 'Come on, Jessica. Sit down and read this.'

I sat in a leather club chair on the other side of the desk, picked up the printout, and held it up to catch the scarce light. It was an article. The headline read: 'STARTLING DEVELOPMENT IN SANTA CLAUS MURDER.'

I glanced up at him. He'd leaned back in his high-back leather chair, fingers laced on his chest, a satisfied smile on his face.

I started to read the article itself.

*   *   *

The brutal murder of a sidewalk Santa Claus on Fifth Avenue a week ago has taken a sudden and dramatic turn. In an exclusive interview with world-famous mystery writer, Jessica Fletcher, this reporter has learned that the individual thought to have been killed that day, Waldo Morse, is, in fact, very much alive.

*   *   *

I slowly shook my head. 'I don't believe you're doing this, Bobby.'

'Keep reading. It gets even better.'

*   *   *

Mrs Fletcher, whose novels about murder have sold in the millions and have been translated into dozens of languages, knew Waldo Morse from her home-town of Cabot Cove, Maine. Morse had run a lobster fishing business out of Ogunquit, Maine, until being arrested for aiding drug smugglers bringing their wares into New England. He copped a plea and, in return for helping convict members of the drug cartel, was placed in the Federal Witness Protection Program. He was in that program when Mrs

225

Fletcher first spotted him across from St. Patrick's Cathedral. She made an appointment to see him the next day. When she returned, she not only witnessed who she thought was Morse being gunned down by unknown assailants, she took photographs of the event. Those photographs ended up in a rival newspaper, an unfortunate fact that has never been explained to anyone by Mrs Fletcher, including the police who would like very much to get their hands on the roll of film.

*   *   *

'This is outrageous,' I said.

'But true, isn't it? Have I misstated any of the facts so far?'

He had. Waldo had not been in the witness protection program when he was working the streets as a charitable Santa. But Johnson wouldn't find that out from me.

I tossed the pages back on the desk.

'You haven't finished,' he said.

'Nor do I intend to. Why are you showing this to me? Obviously, you intend to run this story in your newspaper tomorrow.'

He came forward, causing the springs on his chair to wheeze. He placed his elbows on his desk, laid his chin on a shelf made by his folded hands, and said, 'I don't have to turn this story in, Jessica. That's up to you.'

'If you think I'll change my mind about

doing a book with you, Bobby, you've wasted your valuable writing time. I would certainly prefer that you not run this story, but I would never change my mind in order to avoid that.'

'Fair enough, Jessica. But I don't have to continue sharing information with you, either. I know where Joe Charles is. You say he might be a murderer, and that Morse's wife is in danger because of him. I can nail down that linkup without you.'

I stood and came around the side of the desk. 'I understand how much you want to do this book with me. I don't fault you for that, and maybe I've been too rigid in how I view it. I'm sure you can understand that making such a decision is extremely difficult in the midst of the tension and pressures I've experienced since arriving in New York. I don't make snap decisions, never have. I've often complained that the biggest problem we all face is a lack of quiet, contemplative time to think things out. I promise to give the idea serious consideration once everything has been resolved, and I have an opportunity to go home and clear my head.'

The expression on his face didn't tell me whether I was making an impact or not. I continued. 'If that isn't enough to convince you to take me to Joe Charles tonight, let me again remind you that Nancy Morse's life might be at stake. I believe that Joe Charles knows where she is. If I'm right, confronting him might save her life and the lives of her children.' I raised my hands, then slapped them to my thighs. 'That's all I have to say, Bobby. You can either do what you promised me earlier this evening, take me to where Joe Charles is appearing, or go back on your word, turn in this article, and let the chips fall where they may.' I returned to the living room, picked up my coat from a chair, and put it on.

'Okay,' he said, standing in the doorway. 'But only if you promise one other thing.'

'What's that?'

'That you'll allow me to continue talking to your agent, Russ Checkett. At least give me the opportunity to sell him on the idea.'

'Without me,' I said.

'You said you'd think about it.'

'And I will. Continue talking to him, but only on the condition that you not tell him that I've agreed to anything—yet.'

'Fair enough.'

We had to walk to Broadway to find a cab. When we were ensconced in the backseat of a yellow Checker and Bobby had given the driver an address in the Bronx, I asked how he'd learned where Joe Charles was appearing that evening.

'Easy,' he replied. 'I called the twenty-four-hour jazz line.'

'What's that?'

'A service for the jazz community. You call and get a recording telling you who's appearing in clubs around New York.'

'Just like that,' I said.

'Yeah, just like that.'

'I wish I'd thought of it.'

He laughed. 'But you didn't. Like I said. Jessica, we make a great team.'

CHAPTER TWENTY-TWO

As we left Manhattan and entered the Bronx, the change in landscape was as distinct as the change in my mood. Pure adrenaline had carried me to this stage. I'd been pumped up with a sense of mission. Forget that I'd resolved days ago to leave the digging to Bobby Johnson, and be content with learning from him what had happened. That was then. This was now, a cold, wet night two days before Christmas. I wondered whether Santa visited the Bronx. The real one, I mean. Or, the mythical one. I'm sure he did, at least in the minds of the children. I thought of Santa being murdered on Fifth Avenue, could see the blood again, hear the report of the weapon. I'd never view Santa Claus again in the same pleasant light.

Bobby said little during the ride. He was lost in thought, his attention on the passing scene as we moved through neighborhoods that looked as though they'd suffered massive air raids. I remembered seeing and hearing scenes of the

South Bronx when President Jimmy Carter visited there in 1978. He'd promised to commit a large amount of money to rebuilding the area, but that obviously hadn't happened. So much rebuilding to accomplish and so little money with which to do it. What a tragedy, block after block of such beautiful buildings that once housed thriving families reduced to ruin.

The taxi kept swerving to avoid potholes, but not always successfully. Once, he slammed on the brakes because a painfully thin stray dog darted out in front of us after having knocked over a garbage can. It had started to drizzle before we left Manhattan. The cab's windshield wipers did nothing but smear dirt across the window's surface. The overall impact of the ride was to cause me to almost call a halt to the trip, to instruct the driver to return to Manhattan. Let Bobby Johnson do his stories. I'd had enough.

But then we turned off 137th Street and were on a street called Alexander Avenue. At least there was life there. We passed two magnificent churches and then, to my relief, drove past a police station, in front of which were parked a dozen patrol cars. The movie *Fort Apache* had depicted being a cop in such surroundings. A tough job. Hopefully, our destination wouldn't be too far from the precinct house.

Lights from a couple of small grocery stores

spilled out onto the wet pavement. People milled about in front of them, undeterred by the light rain. Small residential buildings dotted the avenue. It was good to know that other people were there. I'd begun to think Bobby and I were the only two people in the South Bronx that night.

We pulled up in front of a red-brick building. The tattered remains of a green canopy hung loosely over the span between the door and curb. Dozens of garbage cans overflowing with trash stood between us and the door as we exited the cab. Music of the type I'd heard through Joe Charles's door on Crosby Street forced its way to the street. A faint light could be seen through a dirty window, half of which was covered by cardboard. A crude sign written in some sort of pen announced: 'APPEARING TONIGHT JOE CHARLES.'

'This is it, huh?' I said to Bobby as the cab pulled away.

'Looks like it. Not much of a place.'

I looked up and down the street. 'No, it isn't. Let's go in. I'd rather take my chances inside than stand out here.'

The minute we pushed open the door, the music assaulted us with the potency of a tornado. The room was long and narrow. Running along the left side was a bar. Small tables were crowded together along the right-hand side. At the far end of the room was a bandstand on which Joe Charles, surrounded by all his instruments, performed a musical composition that sounded to these untrained ears like a steel factory in full production. It was deafening.

'Over there,' Bobby said, pointing to the only vacant table along the wall. We went to it and, with considerable jockeying, managed to squeeze onto small, rickety wooden chairs. A young woman with a mane of reddish hair, and wearing an extremely short skirt and low-cut blouse, came to our table. Bobby looked at me questioningly. 'Soda,' I shouted. 'Coke or Pepsi.' Bobby ordered a beer. 'No glass, just the bottle,' he said.

The seats we'd taken had me facing the bandstand. Bobby's back was to it. I squinted against tearing eyes. A thick blue haze of smoke filled the room, and there was the pungent odor of marijuana. A young man and woman directly behind Bobby openly passed a cigarette back and forth. I looked to my left and saw that men at the bar had turned to observe us. I suppose it was natural that we would attract attention. Aside from Joe Charles, we seemed to be the only Caucasians in the place.

The waitress placed my soda in front of me, but I didn't touch it. I'd lost my thirst. Talking to Bobby was impossible because of the music's volume, and so we sat, each chewing on our individual thoughts and waiting for Charles to take a blessed intermission.

We must have come in toward the end of his

set because after a crashing finale to whatever composition he was playing, he stopped, nodded to acknowledge the few people who bothered to applaud, stepped down from the bandstand, and went to the bar where he was handed a beer by the barmaid. I was tempted to get up from the table and approach him, but I stayed seated and simply watched. He took a swig from the bottle, wiped his mouth with the back of his hand, and began a conversation with a young woman. It was obviously a pleasant conversation because they laughed a great deal.

'Should we go over to him?' I asked Bobby.

'No. Let's wait a little. I'd rather get him alone.'

My concern was that he would stay with his friend at the bar until it was time to perform again. I wasn't sure my ears could tolerate another round of his music. But then he kissed his friend on the cheek, accepted another beer from the barmaid, and slowly made his way along the bar toward the front door. He was almost abreast of us when he spotted me. I read in his face a combination of surprise, and then panic. 'Joe,' I said, raising my hand.

He stood transfixed, obviously confused about what to do next. Bobby Johnson had turned in his chair so that he faced Charles. 'Can we talk to you for a minute?' he asked.

I sensed Charles was about to turn and head back to the bandstand, or for the door. Bobby and I quickly stood, which placed each of us in the path of either escape route.

'Please, Joe,' I said. 'Give us a few minutes. It's important.'

Our brief dialogue, and the fact we'd stood so suddenly and had him wedged between us, captured the attention of others within earshot. Charles was aware of them looking at us, which, I think, caused him to decide to listen to what we had to say instead of pushing us aside and causing a scene. 'What do you want?' he asked me.

'A few answers, that's all. Please sit down.' I looked about me for a third chair, but there wasn't one.

'Is there another room?' Bobby asked.

'No. Look, I don't know why the hell you came here,' Charles said. 'I don't know anything. I told you that when you came to my apartment, Mrs Fletcher.'

'And I came back, only to find Susan dead. How did she die, Joe?'

My question unnerved him. He started to move away. I put my hand on his arm and said, 'You've got to talk to me. Only for a few minutes.' I looked to the bandstand. 'Could we go up there? I promise I won't take longer than your normal intermission.'

'Yeah, like when you came to my place and said you wouldn't ask any more questions. But you just kept asking them.'

'I'm sorry. A bad habit of mine.'

Charles seemed to be suddenly aware that

Bobby Johnson was there, too. 'Joe,' I said, 'this is Bobby Johnson. He's a reporter.'

From the look on Charles's face, I was sorry I'd mentioned Bobby's press affiliation. 'A reporter? Jesus.'

'Maybe we should go outside,' I suggested.

'Sure,' Charles said. 'Why not?' He heaved a deep sigh, finished what was left of his beer, plunked the empty bottle on the table, and said, 'I could use some air anyway.'

It was raining harder now. We stood beneath the canopy, but its gaping holes afforded little protection. 'Maybe we should go back inside,' I said.

Charles ignored my suggestion and pointed across the street. 'That bodega's open,' he said. He ran across the street, and we followed. It was pleasant and warm inside the small store. An Hispanic husband and wife served customers from behind a counter so laden with items that there was only a small space through which to transact business.

We stood just inside the door. I started to ask a question when the husband behind the counter said something loud in Spanish. He sounded angry.

'Yeah, yeah, *sí sí*,' Charles said. 'He doesn't want us standing here unless we buy something.'

I went to a magazine rack directly behind Charles and pulled out a copy of *El Diario*, the Spanish newspaper. I took it to the counter, paid for it, and returned to Charles and Bobby Johnson. 'This should buy us a few minutes,' I said. 'Joe, do you know where Nancy Morse is?'

'Nancy Morse? Why would I know where she is?'

'Because—she moved from Cabot Cove. I was there the day she left. I think you were there, too.'

He looked at me as though I was crazy. 'You're nuts,' he said. 'Why the hell would I be at her house?'

'You lied to me the day I visited you. You said your phone was broken, but it rang when you were away from the apartment. It was a call from Detective Rizzi.'

'So what? Where's it written that I have to be honest with you?'

'And you and Susan Kale met with him the night I came to Sweet Basil.'

'You didn't *come* to Sweet Basil, Mrs Fletcher. You followed me there.'

'You're right. And then you disappeared.'

'That's also my right. I don't owe you or anybody explanations.'

'Unless you have something to explain.'

'Like what?'

'Like Susan Kale. About why someone tried to kill Waldo on Fifth Avenue.'

'Look, if you think I—wait a minute. *Tried* to kill him?'

'Yes.'

'He *was* killed.'

'No he wasn't. It was someone else that day in the Santa suit.'

'That's ridiculous,' he said.

'I'm surprised you don't know that, Joe. I'm surprised your friend, Detective Rizzi, didn't tell you.'

'He knows?'

'That's a fair assumption.'

'He would have—'

'Would have told you? *Should* have told you?'

He looked down at his shoes. 'Look, Mrs Fletcher, I don't know what to say. All I know is that I'm in a hell of a spot.'

'Why are you in a spot? Knowing that Waldo is alive should be good news. You are his friend, aren't you?'

'Sure I am. How do you know he's alive?'

'Because I've talked with him.'

'Where is he?'

'I'd rather keep that to myself, at least for now. After all, he's in a tough spot, too.' I didn't add that I was afraid what he might do if he knew how to find Waldo.

He noticed that Bobby Johnson had pulled a pad and pencil out of his pocket and was making notes. 'Hey, knock that off,' he said. 'This isn't like some interview.'

'Please, Bobby,' I said. He reluctantly returned the pad and pencil to his pocket.

'I suppose all of this has a logical explanation,' I said, unable to keep the confusion and frustration from my voice. 'But that isn't nearly as important right now as Waldo's wife, Nancy. Is she with you?'

'Of course not. I haven't seen Nancy since high school.'

Could I believe him? For some reason, I did.

'You said she moved,' Charles said. 'Maybe she went out west, or to some foreign country. Why look at me like I should know?'

This time it was the wife who yelled at us in Spanish. I reached for the closest thing, a bag of tortilla chips and held them up to her to see. '*Dinero*,' the wife said. Bobby Johnson swore under his breath, went to the counter, and dug through his pockets for change. While he was there, I asked Joe Charles, 'Did you try to have Waldo killed?'

'What?' He held his hand up in a gesture of sincerity. 'Me? Try to get Waldo killed? Boy, do you have it wrong. Next you'll accuse me of killing Susan. I loved Susan. When you saw me and Rizzi together, and after she was murdered, I figured it was time to split. I'd be in L.A. or Frisco if I had any bread. Why do you think I'm hiding out like this, playing this crummy joint, living in a flophouse? Don't look at me, lady, when you talk about trying to kill somebody. Look at Waldo.'

Johnson returned just as Charles finished his statement. 'What did I just hear, that Waldo Morse is a killer?' he asked.

Charles looked at Johnson. 'I've said
238

enough,' he said.

'But what did you say?' Johnson repeated.

Charles started for the door. Johnson grabbed his arm. Charles turned and looked at me. 'You are some troublemaker, Mrs Fletcher.'

'I am only trying to get to the truth, Joe, and perhaps save Nancy Morse's life. Are you sure you don't know where she is?'

'I don't know, and I don't care. I'm outta here.' With that he was through the door and running across the street.

Johnson looked at me with questioning eyes. 'Come on, Jessica, share with me. Don't forget I brought you here. He claims that Waldo Morse is a murderer?'

I shook my head. 'I don't know what he claims, Bobby. Waldo told me that it might have been Joe Charles who tried to have him killed on the street that day. I asked him about that, which prompted the response you heard. Frankly, I don't know what the truth is.'

'Let's go back and talk to him some more,' Johnson said.

I shook my head. 'He won't say anything else to us. He says he doesn't know where Nancy Morse is.'

'Do you believe him?'

'I think I do. I'm very tired, Bobby. How do we get a cab in this neighborhood?'

'Not easy. Maybe Mom and Pop here will call one for us.'

Johnson returned to the counter where he used pigeon Spanish to get across that we needed a taxi. The wife said, '*Dinero*.' I browsed publications on the magazine rack while waiting for Bobby to return. The door behind me opened. I didn't turn around until the two men who'd entered began shouting in Spanish. When I did turn in response, I was face-to-face with men brandishing handguns. One stayed with me while the other moved quickly to the counter and pointed the weapon at the owners of the store.

I was frozen with fear. At the same time, I broke out into a sweat and my throat went dry. I stared at the man holding a weapon on me. As hard as I tried to avert his stare, I couldn't. His eyes were black and small, and he had the crazed look of someone on drugs.

The voices became louder at the counter. The man with me spun away and ran in that direction. I saw the husband open the register and toss bills on the counter. One of the gunmen scooped them up and shoved them in his pocket.

Then, it happened. There were two shots. I couldn't see who'd been hit. I threw myself to the floor and lay there shaking as two pairs of feet ran from the back of the store toward the door. They stopped for a moment. Did they remember I was there? If they did, they decided not to bother with me because they opened the door and vanished into the night.

The next voices I heard were the husband and wife. Unlike earlier when they were demanding money, they sounded like paid wailers at a funeral. I slowly got to my feet and approached the counter. What I saw affected me as though someone had punched me in the stomach. Lying in a pool of blood was Bobby Johnson.

'Get help,' I said, although I needn't have bothered. The wife had already dialed 911.

I knelt beside Bobby and placed my fingertips on his brow. He was alive; a quick observation indicated that the bullet had hit him in the left shoulder. I pulled a handkerchief from my pocket and pressed it against the wound to stem the flow of blood. 'Just take it easy,' I said. 'Help is on the way. You'll be all right.'

He responded by looking up at me and smiling, actually smiling. And he said, 'Looks like we won't have any problem finding a cab now, Mrs Fletcher.'

CHAPTER TWENTY-THREE

It was déjà vu all over again.

The first two policemen through the door were in uniform. They were followed by none other than Detective Alphonse Rizzi. As had happened on Fifth Avenue, he and his colleagues were there in minutes. Late at night on Alexander Avenue in the South Bronx? It was hardly an area where a detective would be routinely cruising.

'Amazing,' he said.

'It certainly is,' I said. 'Why are you here?'

He gave me one of his patented stupid-question looks and pointed to the rear of the store where an MPD paramedic worked on Bobby Johnson. 'Is that good enough reason for you?'

'That's not what I mean, Detective Rizzi. What I meant was that it seems highly unlikely that you would just happen to be in the area.'

'I'm with Narcotics. This is heavy drug turf.'

'I saw you when I came out of the Pan Am Building earlier this evening.'

'Wrong. The Met Life Building. Pan Am went south.'

'The name of the building doesn't matter. Why are you following me?'

'Don't pride yourself on being important enough to be followed, Mrs Fletcher. I'm not following you.'

'Commissioner Frye said he was withdrawing police escort for me.'

He ignored my comment. 'Who's your friend back there?' he asked.

'His name is Bobby Johnson. He's a *Post* reporter.'

'Oh, that one, the guy who's been turning out all the stories about you.'

'Yes, "that one."'

I went to where the paramedic was tending to Bobby. He'd stopped bleeding, and there was more color in his face. 'It's dangerous hanging around you, Jessica Fletcher,' he said. A laugh accompanied his comment and caused him to cough.

I put my finger to my lips. 'We can talk about that later, Bobby. Right now you just do what you're told and get well.'

An ambulance arrived, and he was removed from the store on a cart. One of the uniformed cops who spoke fluent Spanish interviewed the mom-and-pop owners of the store.

'What hospital is he being taken to?' I asked an EMS technician who'd arrived on the heels of the police.

'Bellevue,' he answered.

'I'd like to accompany him,' I said.

'Against the rules, ma'am.'

Rizzi came up to me. 'I know you like asking all the questions, Mrs Fletcher, but I've got one for you.'

'I'm listening.'

'How come you and the reporter were up here on Alexander Avenue? Not exactly a tourist attraction.'

I hesitated before saying, 'Perhaps the same thing you were doing, Detective. Meeting with Joe Charles across the street.'

I observed his face for a sign of surprise or anger. He demonstrated neither. Nor did he confirm or deny that Joe Charles had been his reason for coming to the South Bronx. I realized, of course, that it was entirely possible that he'd simply followed Bobby and me there. Judging from his actions when we'd left the Wings Club, someone had been following us all night.

'Would you be kind enough to find me a cab?' I asked.

'No need for that, Mrs Fletcher. I'll drive you myself.'

'Directly to my hotel?' I asked.

'Sure, only you'll have to give me a half hour of your time. Since I ended up catching this one, I'll have to get a statement from you.'

'You personally? Why not one of the other officers?'

His face mirrored his frustration with me. 'I've developed sort of an attachment for you,' he said.

'Oh?'

'Yeah. Even though you're a professional thorn in my side, I respect you.'

'Like Mrs Wilson.'

He sort of laughed. 'Yeah, only I wouldn't give her a ride anywhere, at least not if I could help it. Come on, let's go. No sense standing around this dump.'

'It's not a dump,' I said. I went to the counter where the wife was crying. Her husband looked ready to kill. 'Thank you,' I said. 'And *buenos noches*. I think that's the proper term for "good

244

night."'

'*Gracias,*' the husband said. 'Sorry for the trouble.'

I followed Rizzi outside into the rain. He led me to an unmarked vehicle and held open the passenger door. I looked up and down the street before getting in. The shooting had attracted dozens of people, most of whom chattered away in Spanish. It was pouring now. My hair was quickly saturated, which sent rivulets of water down my cheeks and over my nose. I got in the car, and Rizzi closed the door. I wondered if he would put on flashing lights and use his siren, but he didn't. He drove slowly and quietly through the rubble-strewn streets and into less ravaged Manhattan.

'You know, Mrs Fletcher. I'm really not a bad guy. You just see one side of me.'

'I never considered you a bad guy, Detective.'

'There's a lot you don't know about me.'

More than you realize, I thought. I said, 'Well, I know that you appreciate and understand fine wine and art. I know that you're married, that your wife's name is Emily, and that you have a mother-in-law named Mrs Wilson.'

'I don't mean that kind of stuff. I mean about being a cop. Where is it you live?'

'Cabot Cove, Maine.'

'A little town, huh?'

'Yes.'

245

'You see, Mrs Fletcher, this is different than what you know about. Here in New York you don't police by the book. Can't. It doesn't matter what all the knee-jerk liberals say about respecting individual rights. It doesn't work. The scum on the street look at cops like we're idiots, jerks. We arrest them, the judges let 'em go. We protect ourselves and we're brought up on charges and the public wants our heads. You understand what I'm saying?'

'I think so.'

'You cut corners if you want to be a good cop—and live to write a book about it.'

'Is that what you want to do, write a book about your years as a police officer?'

'I wouldn't mind.'

'I'm sure it will be a very good book.'

We pulled up to the curb in front of the Sheraton-Park Avenue. He turned off the ignition and faced me. 'You mind if I come in, Mrs Fletcher. I could take a statement here in the car but it's too cold.'

'Of course.'

I suggested we sit in a quiet corner of the empty lobby, but he shook his head. 'Too public, Mrs Fletcher. If you don't mind, I'd just as soon come up to your room.'

'Well, I—'

'Not to worry, Mrs Fletcher. I haven't raped anybody in years.' He chuckled at his little joke.

Rape was the furthest thing from my mind, but I didn't express it. I said instead, 'All right.

let me make a fast phone call first.' I went to a house phone and dialed the room shared by Mort and Seth. They didn't answer, and the operator came on the line. 'This is Jessica Fletcher in the penthouse suite. Please leave a message for Sheriff Metzger and Dr Hazlitt. Tell them I'm meeting in my suite with Detective Rizzi. And be sure to indicate the time of this call.'

'I hope this will be brief,' I said when Rizzi and I walked into the suite. 'I'm exhausted. Excuse me. I see that my message light is flashing, and I want to call the hospital to check on Bobby Johnson.'

'Do that after I'm gone, Mrs Fletcher,' Rizzi said. 'You said you wanted this quick. That suits me, too.'

'All right.' I removed my coat and sat in a chair. 'Do you want me to make a statement, or do you wish to ask questions?'

Rizzi's response was interrupted by a violent sneeze. Then another. A third came immediately.

'Bless you,' I said.

'You got a cat up here?'

I laughed. 'As a matter of fact, I do. Miss Hiss. I rescued her from that apartment where Susan Kale was murdered.'

He pulled out a handkerchief and wiped eyes that had begun to run. 'I got a terrible allergy to cats, Mrs Fletcher.'

'We should have stayed downstairs.'

'Mrs Wilson bought two cats just to make me miserable.'

'Oh.'

'Where is the cat?'

'In the bathroom.' The bathroom door was slightly ajar. Miss Hiss pushed through it and headed directly for Rizzi. He quickly stood and walked to the other side of the room. The cat continued in his direction. 'Please, Mrs Fletcher, get that thing away from me.'

I picked her up, put her back in the bathroom, and closed the door. 'Better?' I asked.

'No, but go ahead. Tell me what happened tonight, why you were there, what you saw.'

Had I not mentioned Joe Charles when we talked at the scene of the shooting, I would not have mentioned him now. But since I already had, I started with an explanation of how Bobby Johnson had found Joe Charles playing in the small dive across from the bodega, and that we'd gone there to speak with him.

'Speak with him about what?'

'About—'

Rizzi went into a sneezing frenzy. He managed to ask in the midst of it, 'You got another bathroom in this place? Sometimes water on my face helps.'

I pointed him in the direction of the second bath. While he was gone, I decided to retrieve my messages. There were calls from Vaughan Buckley, Ruth Lazzara, Seth and Morton earlier in the evening and, finally, the message left by Nancy Morse. 'Are you sure she didn't leave any way to reach her?' I asked the operator.

'Afraid not, Mrs Fletcher. I asked, but she said she would call back.'

'Thank you.'

I wrote down on a pad the name of each caller and left it next to the phone. Rizzi returned from the bathroom. I excused myself to make a different use than he had of the same facility. I reached the door and looked back. He was leaning over the pad scrutinizing the names I had written.

When I returned, he had his topcoat on and was about to leave.

'I thought you wanted a statement from me,' I said.

'I got enough from this visit, Mrs Fletcher. Somebody'll get in touch with you tomorrow to take a formal statement. In the meantime, stay out of bad neighborhoods. You can get hurt in them.'

CHAPTER TWENTY-FOUR

My call to Bellevue Hospital had confirmed that Bobby Johnson was doing nicely. His condition was listed as 'satisfactory.' I returned the other calls. Seth and Morton had taken in a Broadway show. To my surprise, Mort had loved it but Seth found it 'lacking in artistic integrity and dramatic urgency.' Usually, Mort has trouble sitting through even a half-hour television show, and invariably finds all dramatic presentations silly at best, subversive at worst.

Naturally, my call informing them that I was being interrogated by Rizzi in my suite triggered a barrage of questions about my evening and what had led up to being questioned. 'Just routine,' I told them. The thought of recounting my adventure in the South Bronx was too painful, so I didn't. I focused on the parties and dinner, summing up the rest of the evening with, 'There are so many areas to explore in New York. You see something new and interesting everywhere you look.'

Vaughan Buckley simply wanted to tell me how I'd charmed Wolfgang Wurtzman, and that he and Olga were looking forward to having me at their Christmas Eve party the following evening. Ruth Lazzara, of course, was simply confirming the next day's activities, which would begin with a ten-o'clock book signing at Macy's. I asked her for a phone number at which I could be reached at the store. She called back with it a few minutes later. I then called information on Long Island and got the number for K. C. Gallaghers in Sea Cliff. Should Nancy Morse call again, I wanted the operator to have every possible number at which I could be reached.

I slept well considering everything that had happened. I had breakfast in the room, enjoyed a leisurely shower, and felt rested and relaxed when it was time to meet Ruth in the lobby for our trip to Macy's. Because public scrutiny of my daily activities had diminished, I'd become used to arriving in the lobby without being ambushed by the press. Which accounted for my surprise when I stepped off the elevator and was confronted with cameras and reporters. I was about to retreat to the security of the elevator when Ruth, who'd been hidden behind a group of media representatives, yelled my name and ran to me. 'This is incredible,' she said, thrusting a copy of that morning's *New York Post* at me. The entire front page was covered with a stock photograph of me. A small insert picture in the lower right-hand corner was of the bodega's entrance. The headline—it couldn't have been bigger—read: 'JESS DOES IT AGAIN!'

I pulled Ruth into the elevator and pushed the button for my floor. Reporters tried to join us, but I held them off with a steely stare.

'I can't believe this happened to you last night,' Ruth said. 'Why didn't you tell me when you called?'

'Because I wanted to forget about it,' I said, turning to Page Three where the story began. It was bylined by, who else? Bobby Johnson 'reporting from his bed at Bellevue Hospital.'

He recounted the details of the shooting and made much of the fact that I was witness to yet another Manhattan assault. The rest of the story was dominated by a rehash of the Santa Claus slaying on Fifth Avenue, my discovering the body of Susan Kale, and the fact that we'd gone to the South Bronx to talk to a musician, Joe Charles, in the hope of verifying that the person originally thought to have died in the Santa Claus costume had not, in fact, been that person. At least he'd fudged it. He hadn't claimed outright that Waldo Morse was alive.

When we were in the suite, I said, 'This is dreadful.'

'I know,' Ruth said without conviction. 'It must be trying for you. But the publicity is incredible. Johnson mentions the name of your new book at least three times. And he calls you "Manhattan's Mayhem Madam."' She giggled.

I winced.

The phone rang. It was Seth, who'd just picked up the *Post*. 'You stay right there, Jessica. Mort and I are on our way up.'

'I can't face the press again,' I said to Ruth.

'Is there a back door?' she asked.

I thought of my previous escape from the roof and down to the kitchen, but thought better of it. There was a loud knock on the door. I opened it, and Seth and Morton came in. Seth wore his usual brown tweed jacket, forest green suede vest, and bow tie. Morton, no surprise, was in his tan Cabot Cove sheriff's

252

uniform replete with badge, and broad-brimmed Stetson hat.

'We have to go,' Ruth said.

'Where are we going?' Morton asked.

'Macy's,' I said. 'To sign books.'

'If it was me, Jessica, I'd cancel out and stay right here,' said Seth. 'Not safe for you to be out on the streets of this city.'

I forced a laugh. 'Don't be silly,' I said. 'The only threat to me is the free press. If you gentlemen will run interference for me, I'm ready to leave.'

They did a pretty good job of helping me navigate the crowd in the lobby and out to the sidewalk. We were followed of course, as we made our way across town to Macy's on Thirty-fourth Street, but the store's management did a good job of crowd control. They kept the press at bay while I frantically signed books for hundreds of people.

I'd ordered a car to pick me up in front of the store at eleven-thirty. Seth, Morton, and Ruth accompanied me out to the sidewalk where I found my driver, who held up a large cardboard sign with my name on it.

'Where are you going?' Ruth asked.

'A personal errand,' I said.

Seth opened the back door and climbed in.

'Where are *you* going?' I asked.

'With you on this personal errand,' he said. 'Come on, get in.'

Two things crossed my mind. The first was

that there was no way I could dissuade them from accompanying me. The second was that I welcomed their company. I was naturally concerned that their presence might upset Waldo. But it wasn't as though I was bringing total strangers. They'd known Waldo's mother in Cabot Cove. If being with me bothered Waldo, so be it. It was time I stopped doing a solo act.

'By the way,' Morton said as we headed for the Queens Midtown Tunnel and the Long Island Expressway, 'I got hold of the moving company in Portland that moved Nancy.'

I looked at him with wide eyes. 'And?'

'Seems they brought her here to New York City.'

I wasn't surprised, not with the message she'd left at the hotel. Of course, she could have called long distance, but somehow I doubted it. I asked, 'What address did they take her to?'

Morton pulled a slip of paper from his pocket and handed it to me. It was a building number on Sullivan Street. 'Thanks, Mort,' I said. 'I appreciate this.'

I've heard people refer to the Long Island Expressway as the world's longest parking lot. I was now a believer. It was a tortuous ride to where we exited and headed north until reaching the quaint, petite village of Sea Cliff. It was lovely, an oasis not many miles from Manhattan that reminded me somewhat of

254

Cabot Cove. It was on the water, Long Island Sound, and the houses were gingerbready and eclectic. Our driver let us out across the street from K. C. Gallagher's, an unimposing storefront pub with small evergreens decorated with red Christmas bows in window boxes.

'Cute place,' Seth said. A young couple passed and gave Mort and his uniform a second look.

'Think he'll show up?' Seth asked.

'There's one way to find out,' I said.

Waldo was seated at a table for two in a back corner. He saw me come through the door and started to stand, then saw Seth and Mort and sat back down. I quickly went to him because I knew what he was thinking. 'Waldo,' I said, placing a hand on his shoulder, 'it's all right. These are friends from Cabot Cove. We're *all* here to help you.'

His expression said he wasn't sure. But he didn't leave.

'We'll need a bigger table,' I said.

We took a vacant table for four in the opposite corner. Waldo obviously was no stranger to the restaurant. A waitress immediately appeared and asked if he would have 'his usual.' We all ended up ordering it, French onion soup and salads.

'I don't like this,' Waldo said after the waitress had left the table. 'Who are you people?'

I explained Mort and Seth's connection to

255

me. 'Mort learned where Nancy might have moved,' I said.

'Where?'

'Seems they moved some of her things to a place called Sullivan Street,' Mort replied.

I added, 'Nancy tried to reach me last night, but I wasn't at the hotel when she called. She didn't leave a number. Have you seen the papers this morning?'

'The *Times*.'

'There's a front-page story in the *Post* about an incident in which I was involved last night. A reporter, Bobby Johnson, was shot in a store in the Bronx. I was with him. He wrote about it from his hospital room. He mentions in the article that there is the possibility you are still alive.'

'Great,' Waldo said. 'That's just great. How did he find that out?'

'From me, I'm afraid. But I don't think it will matter if we move quickly. I also saw Joe Charles last night.'

'Where?'

'At a small jazz club across from the store where the reporter was shot.'

'Was Nancy—?'

'No, she wasn't with him. That's why I went to see him, to ask if he knew her whereabouts. He said he didn't.'

'You believe him?'

'Yes.'

'I hope you're right, Mrs Fletcher. He's

dangerous. He'll do anything to save his hide.'

'What's he have to save himself from?' Mort asked in his best interrogation voice.

'He—he's a drug runner,' Waldo replied.

'He is?' My surprise was genuine.

Waldo looked at Seth and Mort before asking me. 'Are you sure I can talk freely?'

I nodded. 'Trust me, Waldo. Trust us.'

'Okay. I don't know why I should, but I'm running out of options. If what you say is true about people knowing I'm alive, I might not stay that way very long.'

'Go on, Waldo. Tell us about Joe Charles.'

He gathered his thoughts before saying. 'When I split from the witness protection program and started working for New York MPD, one of my first assignments was to link up with Joe again. The cops knew he was dealing drugs, especially in the jazz community. Turns out some of his suppliers are connected with the guys I helped put away. Joe was sort of a conduit for musicians, a guy they could always come to make a buy. Rizzi—'

'That's the detective assigned to Waldo,' I explained to my friends. 'And he's been assigned to me in a manner of speaking. Go on Waldo.'

'Yeah, Mrs Fletcher's right,' he said. 'Rizzi has been my control ever since I started informing. Anyway, when Rizzi found out that Joe and I went back to Cabot Cove together, he set me on to him. We got friendly again, only it

257

wasn't exactly friendship. I mean, I was hanging around with him and then telling Rizzi everything about how Joe dealt drugs, who bought them, stuff like that. I was a rat, a well-paid one.'

Morton's expression said he'd just tasted something sour. But Seth leaned closer to Waldo and said, 'Sometimes we do what we have to do, Waldo. I got a feeling that this Joe Charles came to know what you were doin' to him.'

'That's right.'

'Did Joe know you'd arranged to have your friend stand in for you that day?' I asked.

'I don't think so. At least he didn't learn it from me.'

'What about Susan Kale?' I said. 'She told me she'd lived with you and with Joe Charles at different times. And you indicated at the library that you thought Joe might have killed her. Why?'

'For the same reason he wanted me out of the way. Susan came to know what was going on between me and Joe. Knowing too much about double-dealing isn't healthy. At least not in this case.'

I told Waldo about having seen Joe Charles. Susan Kale, and Detective Rizzi together at Sweet Basil. 'If Rizzi and the police were interested in Joe because he was a drug dealer, why would the detective and the drug runner be together in a jazz club?' I asked.

'Because—' Waldo looked to Mort Metzger before completing his statement. 'Because Rizzi's dirty.'

'Dirty?'

'Yes. Dirty.'

'Careful now accusing a law enforcement officer,' Mort said sternly.

'I can't prove it,' Waldo said. 'But talk on the street is that Rizzi is always on the take, always with his hand out to drug dealers in return for looking the other way.'

'You wouldn't see any 'a that in Cabot Cove,' Mort said.

'Waldo,' said Seth, 'did this Detective Rizzi become aware that *you* know he's "dirty" as you put it?'

The soup and salads were served. Waldo answered Seth. 'I have no way of knowing,' he said. 'I suppose the guys who told me might have told Rizzi I know about him. *I* sure never brought it up with him.'

'But he knows that you dropped out of the federal program,' I offered. 'He might assume you're ready to do the same with him and the New York police. If you did—if you were no longer under his thumb—you might be tempted to talk to another authority.'

Waldo started to respond but I quickly added, 'And consider this, Waldo. Rizzi didn't know about the switch that day between you and your friend. At least he wouldn't have known about it until after the fact. Once he did

259

realize it, it could have been the subject of the conversation I witnessed between Joe, Susan, and Rizzi that night in Sweet Basil. I know one thing for certain. They weren't happy about something.'

We fell silent. Seth twisted some of the melted cheese from the top of his soup and tasted it. Food had no appeal for me at that moment. Morton's soup and salad were almost gone.

'Excuse me,' Waldo said. 'Nature calls.'

He went behind a partition and was out of our sight.

'What do you think?' I asked Mort and Seth.

'Hard to say,' Mort replied. 'Can't say I like him much. Anybody gets involved with drugs like he did doesn't sit well with me, no matter what excuses they make.'

'Do you believe him?' I asked.

'That's hard to say, too,' said Seth. 'You get one story from Joe Charles, another from him. Some friends. Seems like they're each out to sink the other.'

'Exactly what I was thinking,' I said. 'But what if both are telling the truth? I mean, at least from their individual perspectives? Somehow, Detective Alphonse Rizzi keeps coming to mind. No offense, Morton, but being a police officer doesn't necessarily mean he's a good person.'

'Are you suggestin' that this Detective Rizzi might actually have tried to kill Waldo, and kill
260

that girl, too?' Seth asked.

I sat back and closed my eyes, slowly shook my head. 'I can't prove it, but I have this nagging feeling that he's capable of it. Waldo says Rizzi is dirty, that he takes payoffs from drug dealers. If that's true, he'd have every reason to get rid of people who knew about it and could testify against him.'

'Soup is good,' Seth said, taking another spoonful.

I glanced at my watch. Waldo had been gone too long. I mentioned it to Seth and Morton.

Mort wiped his mouth with his napkin. 'I'll go check on him,' he said, hitching up his pants and following Waldo's footsteps. He returned moments later. 'I can't find him,' he said.

I motioned for our waitress. 'Did you see where Waldo went?' I asked.

She smiled. 'Looks like he did what he usually does,' she said. 'I think you're stuck with the check.' She handed it to Seth.

'By the old Lord Harry!' Seth muttered.

'Shiftless son-of-a-gun,' Mort said.

'Why would he have run from us?' I asked aloud. 'Where would he be going in such a hurry?'

I picked up the check that Seth had dropped on the table. 'I'll get this,' I said. 'We'd better head back to the city.' I took a credit card from my purse and laid it on the check. It was then that I noticed that the waitress had left a pencil with it. A plain, old-fashioned Number Two

261

lead pencil.

I went back into my purse and found the sheets of paper I'd taken from the yellow legal pad in Nancy Morse's kitchen in Cabot Cove. I pushed aside the tablecloth on my side and laid the pages on the table's hard surface.

'What the devil are you doin'?' Seth asked.

'Something I've been meaning to do ever since we went to Nancy's house.' I held the pencil so that the side of the lead was flat and began to slowly rub it over the faint indentations on the paper. Words began to appear. They were barely readable, but when the paper was held to catch the light at precisely the right angle, they took shape.

Seth and Morton moved next to me and squinted to read what had formed on the paper. Not every word took shape, but enough had for the message to come through loud and clear.

I shoved the pages back in my purse, replaced my credit card with enough cash to cover the bill and stood. 'Come on,' I said. 'We don't have a minute to lose.'

CHAPTER TWENTY-FIVE

Sullivan Street, according to our talkative driver, was actually in Greenwich Village but was sometimes considered part of New York's

Little Italy. It was a lovely street of row houses that had been renovated over the years. But even with attempts at modernization, it retained the look of yesteryear, a set Hollywood might build for a movie about turn-of-the-century immigrants in Manhattan.

We stopped in front of the address Morton had gotten from the moving company. 'What now?' Seth asked.

'Let's see if she's put her name on one of the mail-boxes,' I suggested. I knew she wouldn't have if seeking anonymity, but it was worth a try. I went up the short flight of steps and checked. No Morse. I returned to the car. 'No luck,' I said. 'I guess we just wait. Is that all right with you?' I asked the driver.

'I'm yours till six,' he said. 'I go off-duty then. It's Christmas Eve.'

'It certainly is,' I said. A wave of nostalgia swept over me. Sitting in a hired car on a Greenwich Village street was a new holiday experience for me, one I hoped would never be repeated.

'Want me to go in and knock on a few doors?' Mort asked.

'No, let's just sit here awhile,' I said. 'We'll give it a half hour.'

As we waited, the sunshine of earlier in the day was replaced with low, angry clouds from which snow began to fall, gently at first but then whipped by a sudden wind into a horizontal whiteout. People on the street reacted predictably, walking faster, coats pulled up tight around their necks, hats pulled lower over their foreheads. Those walking into the wind leaned forward. Everyone seemed to be carrying presents wrapped in brightly colored paper. Lights on Christmas trees and wreaths in apartment windows took on their own surrealistic movement as the driven snow whipped past them. The sound of the wind, and of the car's heater, was embellished by a church bell from across the street.

'Like some Christmas music?' the driver asked, turning on the radio before we had a chance to answer.

'Wait,' I said.

'Huh?' the driver said.

'Turn it off,' I said.

'Sounds pretty,' Seth said.

The driver clicked off the radio. I leaned forward and peered through the window. It wasn't easy to see because of the weather, but there was no doubt that it was Waldo coming up the street. He was moving fast, hunched forward into the wind, hands jammed in the pockets of his army surplus jacket, eyes narrowed against the sting of the snow.

'Here comes Waldo,' I said.

Mort and Seth turned to see what I was seeing. 'Ayuh, that's him all right,' said Seth.

Waldo walked past us and stopped at the building to which Nancy had moved, hesitated, looked left and right, went up the steps and disappeared inside.

'Looks like you were right, Jess,' Seth said. 'He knew exactly what building it was.' I'd told Waldo only that Nancy had moved to Sullivan Street. I hadn't given him the address. I also knew why he'd run from the restaurant in Sea Cliff. My acknowledgement that I knew where Nancy was had panicked him. The note I'd deciphered, written to him by Nancy, told me only that he and Nancy were planning to run off together. It didn't tell me when. My assumption was that the timetable would be pushed up, which proved out.

'I'll go get him,' Mort said, reaching for the door handle.

'Wait,' I said. 'Look.'

A car driven by Detective Alphonse Rizzi, the same car he'd driven me in the previous night, parked at a hydrant up the street. Rizzi got out, went straight to the building, and bounded up the steps.

'Who's that?' Seth asked.

'The infamous Detective Rizzi,' I said. 'Let's go.'

The three of us left the car and walked quickly to where Rizzi stood at the top of the steps. He'd just pressed one of the buzzers, and the return buzz that allowed the door to be opened sounded. 'Hello,' I said.

He looked down at me. For the first time since I'd met him, his expression wasn't one of anger or scorn. He was surprised, pure and simple. I went up the steps with Seth and Morton at my side. 'I know why you're here,' I said. 'Waldo Morse has already arrived. I assume he's with his wife, Nancy.'

The buzzing had stopped. Now it started again. 'Is that you, Rizzi?' Waldo's voice asked through a tiny speaker. 'Come on up.'

'Get out of here,' Rizzi said to me.

'Morton Metzger, sheriff of Cabot Cove, Maine,' Morton said, flashing his ID.

'Detective Rizzi,' I said, 'we're not going anywhere until I talk to Nancy Morse.' The buzzer sounded angrier this time. So did Waldo. 'Hey, is that you, Rizzi? Come on, we don't have all day.'

I stepped past him and pushed open the door. If he had any thoughts of stopping me, the presence of Seth and Mort laid them to rest. I turned to him and said, 'What apartment is it, Detective? We'll bang on every door if we have to.'

'All right, Mrs Fletcher. You're here. You might as well go up. But don't say I didn't warn you.'

'*We'll* go up,' I said, nodding at Seth and Morton.

'Two C,' Rizzi said.

I led the way, with Rizzi bringing up the rear. The door to Apartment Two C was at the top of the stairs and open. Waldo stood in it. 'Hey, what are you doing here?' he said when he saw me.

266

'Putting an end to the unpleasant part of my trip to New York,' I replied. I was angry, and my voice testified to it.

'Who is it?' Nancy asked as she came to the door. 'Mrs Fletcher. How did you—?'

'It doesn't matter how I found you, Nancy. May we come in?' I looked back at Rizzi, who shrugged at Waldo and Nancy.

The apartment was virtually bare. A metal single bed was against one wall. Two directors' chairs were against another. Suitcases were piled near the door.

Waldo and Nancy didn't appear to be ready to move to allow us to enter, but when Morton stepped toward them, they backed inside. We all entered. Waldo and Nancy stood together in front of their suitcases. They held hands.

'You knew where Nancy was all along,' I said to Waldo. 'This was planned from the beginning, your staged murder, Nancy's sudden move from Cabot Cove, everything—except for Susan Kale.'

'What do you mean by that?' Waldo asked.

'What I mean, Waldo, is that you didn't include murdering her in your plans. The only murder you arranged for was your unfortunate friend, George Marsh.'

'I think you've said enough, Mrs Fletcher,' Rizzi said.

'I disagree,' I responded. 'You were in on it, too, from the beginning. You knew Waldo was setting up to disappear, and that feigning his

267

own death was the first step.'

I looked to Nancy, who'd disengaged her hand from Waldo's and stepped away from him. I asked her, 'Nancy, did you know that Waldo intended to have someone killed in order that people should think he'd died?'

She looked at Rizzi as though wanting him to answer my question. I, too, looked at him. 'I don't understand,' I said to the detective, 'why you would be a part of this. You're supposed to uphold the law, not help someone break it.'

'You're in over your head, Mrs Fletcher,' Rizzi replied. 'I tried to give you a lesson last night in how the real world works in New York. You and your buffoon friends here think the world works like in your little town in Maine. The fact is, I do what needs to be done to get results. You deal from theories. You write nice, neat little books about murder where the bad guys wear black hats and the good guys wear the white ones. Everything tied up at the end. Crime doesn't pay. The killer gets his, and the good guys ride off into the sunset together. Sorry. It don't work that way in real life.'

I turned to Waldo and Nancy. 'Is that what you're trying to do, "ride off into the sunset together" as Detective Rizzi puts it?'

'What's wrong with that?' Nancy asked, steeping forward, her chin jutting out at me. 'Don't you think we've paid enough? You haven't lived my life all these years, Mrs Fletcher. It's been a living hell for me and the kids. This was a chance to put it all back together, for Waldo and me and the kids to start over. Yes, I knew what Waldo planned to do.'

'Shut up, Nancy,' Waldo said.

'No, *you* shut up! We've been put in this position because of you and your stupidity in Ogunquit.' She smiled at me. 'The fact is, Mrs Fletcher, it doesn't matter what you and your friends know because everything that's happened has the blessing of the New York City Police Department. Everything. Isn't that right, Detective Rizzi?'

'She's right, Mrs Fletcher. Like I said, you don't understand the real world. You think of yourself as a nice person. Right? A real lady who cuddles little animals and wants everybody in the world to live happily ever after. You want these two people to live like that? Then get lost. Go back to your cocoon in Maine and take these guys with you. So somebody gets killed, like this loser in the Santa Claus getup. Because 'a that, Waldo and Nancy get to see that sunset. He's done a good job for us, paid his dues. But now it's time for him to move on. I like that. A nice happy ending for the book I write when I retire.'

'And a life—two lives—mean nothing to accomplish this.'

'You ready?' Rizzi said to Waldo and Nancy. They answered by beginning to pick up the suitcases.

I stood there feeling more helpless than ever before in my life. It was the way I'd felt on Fifth Avenue the day George Marsh was shot, the callous attitude of witnesses to the slaying, the nonchalant air of Rizzi and the other police. Helpless. What was I to do? What *could* I do? Waldo Morse, with the blessing of his wife, had arranged for a friend to be murdered in order that he and Nancy might be free to flee their current lives for a new and better one. There they were, willing to admit it and about to head for an airport or train station—and a New York City detective was helping them.

'What about Susan Kale?' I asked, my voice reflecting how little time I had to ask anything. 'What did she do to deserve to die, threaten to expose your scheme? Or did she get in the way because she loved you, Waldo?'

'Grab that other bag,' Nancy told Rizzi, who did.

'You even carry their luggage,' I said. 'How pathetic.'

I looked at Seth and Morton. 'I'm an officer of the law,' Mort said. 'There's a murder been admitted to here.'

'Cool it, Sheriff,' Rizzi said. 'You might be a law enforcement officer in Maine, but here you're nothin'. Get out of the way.'

The three of us stepped back and allowed them to leave, saw them struggle down the stairs with their bags, watched as they put the luggage in the trunk of Rizzi's car, get in themselves, pull away from the curb, and never look back.

'Must be somethin' we can do,' Seth said.

'I'm afraid there isn't,' I said sadly. 'Except to go home.'

CHAPTER TWENTY-SIX

My favorite day of the year has always been New Year's Day. It's a day of pure relaxation, as well as the official beginning of a new year and what it promises.

But this New Year's Day had even greater meaning for me. The previous year had ended on its sad, frustrating note on Sullivan Street in New York City. Hopefully, the new year would be full and rich enough to smother lingering memories of it.

Seth, Morton, and I had attended the Buckleys' Christmas Eve party at their apartment, although we didn't stay very long. I'd taken Vaughan aside earlier in the evening and told him what had happened that afternoon. He was shocked, of course. 'Please don't let this put a damper on your party,' I said. 'I'd just as soon that no one aside from you and Olga know about it. And, Vaughan, I'm afraid I must change my plans. My friends and I want to go back to Cabot Cove in the morning. I know it means canceling a few

271

promotional appearances next week, but there really aren't many.'

'Of course,' he said. 'I do hope you'll find some time to tell me the story in more detail.'

'Maybe one day,' I said. 'But what I really want is to forget it as quickly as possible.'

Seth, Morton, and I took a flight on Christmas morning to Boston. Jed Richardson met us in one of his twin-engine aircraft, and flew us without incident to Cabot Cove.

And here it was New Year's Day. I was in my favorite sweatsuit. A fire crackled in the fireplace. I'd attended the annual Cabot Cove New Year's Eve party but hadn't stayed late at that, either. I was asleep by eleven; the new year rolled in without me.

Seth, Morton, and a few other close friends planned to stop by later in the afternoon to share in the clam pies I'd ordered from Charlene Sassi. It was noon. I was at my desk going through the last of a mound of mail that had accumulated while I was away when the phone rang.

'Hello?'

'Jessica. Bobby Johnson.'

'Bobby. How are you?'

'Fine. Healing up great. You?'

'All right.'

'I've got some interesting news, Jess.'

'You have my undivided attention,' I said.

'I took everything I have on Rizzi, Waldo, Joe Charles, the works to my publisher. It took him a while to decide what to do, but he finally set me up with an assistant Manhattan D.A. I figured nobody would take action against a cop like Rizzi, but I was wrong. This D.A.—she's a tough lady, Jess, you'd really like her—is calling for a grand jury hearing on the whole ball 'a wax. She's got subpoenas out for Waldo, Nancy, and Joe Charles. Rizzi's been suspended pending an Internal Affairs investigation. Jess, I think they're all going to go down.' The enthusiasm in his voice was contagious and satisfying.

'That's wonderful news,' I said.

'Yeah. I thought you'd want to know. I also called to wish you a happy new year, Jess, and to thank you for what you did with Russ Checkett.'

'I didn't do anything.'

'Sure you did. If it wasn't for you, I don't think he would have taken me on as a client and agreed to represent *The Santa Claus Murder*.'

'I'm sure it will be a very good and successful book, especially if Rizzi and the others "go down," as you put it.'

'Russ told me you agreed to read the manuscript and consider providing an endorsement to use on the cover and in ads.'

'Yes, I did. Happy to, Bobby.'

I fell silent.

'Jess?'

'Yes, sorry. My mind was wandering. I was

273

thinking that Rizzi was right. I don't deal with the real world of crime, especially the way it's played out in New York.'

'Don't feel bad about not understanding it, Jess. It isn't to be understood except by the players. Still willing to have me come up for a couple of days so I can drag all you remember out of you?'

'I have to think about that, Bobby.'

'Use that quiet time you crave to contemplate?'

'Something like that. It was good of you to call, and I'm glad you're on the mend. Happy new year.'

'Same to you, Jessica Fletcher. You're some special lady.'

The evening was quiet and lovely. The clam pies were unusually tasty, the conversation subdued and pleasant. Everyone left by nine except for Mort and Seth. They lingered for an extra cup of coffee. As we sat in my kitchen, the subject of Waldo Morse came up for the first time that night. 'The level of deception Waldo Morse practiced is remarkable to me,' Seth said. 'To think that he could fake his own death and then disappear indicates how unbalanced he is.'

'And cruel,' I added. 'Having his friend stand in for him, knowing he'd be killed, was horrible. But I'm afraid Waldo has been practicing deception his entire life. In some perverted way, he meant well. He wanted to get out of the life he'd been leading and accomplish what he'd intended when he became a witness against those drug dealers in Maine. He wanted to go somewhere with his wife and children, and establish a quiet life. But he wasn't the only one practicing deception. The people he put his faith in weren't honorable or honest, either.'

'I feel especially sorry for that young girl,' Mort said, taking another piece of apple pie I'd baked that morning. 'She just ended up in the wrong place at the wrong time.'

'More important, she hung out with the wrong sort 'a fellas,' Seth said. 'Like I always say, if you want a good life, hang out with the winners.'

'In her case, the lesson is if you want to *live*,' I said.

'The amazing thing is that Waldo didn't kill you, Jess,' Mort said. 'When you showed up on Fifth Avenue that day and recognized him, you upset his whole misguided scheme.'

'I've thought of that on occasion but I try not to dwell upon it.' I told them what Bobby Johnson had told me, that it looked as though Rizzi, Waldo, Nancy, and Joe Charles would have to face a jury one day for their deeds.

'I hope so,' Mort said. 'Just wouldn't seem right that no justice comes out of what they did, two murders and all.'

I smiled, said, 'Somehow, gentlemen, I believe that justice will prevail in their case no matter how this district attorney fares in prosecuting them. I'm talking about the brand of justice in which the guilty live a life in their own private Hell.'

'Like *No Exit*,' Seth said.

'What's that?' Mort asked.

'A play by Jean Paul Sartre,' Seth said. 'He defined Hell as being in a locked room with people you can't stand. Maybe that's what Waldo and his wife will suffer.'

'I think you're right, Seth,' I said. 'There's no exit from the life they'll be living for the rest of their lives. By the way, Mort, how is Miss Hiss?'

'Cute little rascal. Gets along real good with Jesse.' Jesse was Mort's dog. He swears he didn't name her after me, but I've always had my doubts. He'd agreed to take Miss Hiss, and the adoption was working out fine.

I started to laugh.

'What's funny?' asked Seth.

'I was just thinking of the night Rizzi came to my hotel suite and started sneezing. He's very allergic to cats, and Miss Hiss really set him off. He told me that his mother-in-law, Mrs Wilson, who evidently is no fan of his, bought two cats just to torture him. That's how I see justice being dispensed where he's concerned. Locked in a room with a thousand cats and no exit.'

They laughed, too. 'I kind 'a like that, Jess,' Mort said.

'So do I,' said Seth.

'I thought you would. Now go home. This

writer starts her new book first thing in the morning.'

*   *   *

I learned later that charges were brought against Rizzi, Waldo Morse, and Joe Charles. Nancy Morse wasn't indicted, although she'd certainly been a co-conspirator in Waldo's twisted scheme. The three of them had been found in a little town in New Mexico where they lived together. I felt bad for Nancy's children. The sins of their father would certainly impact upon their young lives.

Hopefully, Bobby Johnson's book about what became known as the Santa Claus Murder will shed light on what really happened, especially Detective Alphonse Rizzi's role in it. I fervently hope so, as much as I hope that one day I'll be able to forget about it. I think the former is realistic. As for my latter wish, only time will tell.

We hope you have enjoyed this Large Print book. Other Chivers Press or G.K. Hall & Co. Large Print books are available at your library or directly from the publishers.

For more information about current and forthcoming titles, please call or write, without obligation, to:

Chivers Press Limited
Windsor Bridge Road
Bath BA2 3AX
England
Tel. (01225) 335336

OR

G.K. Hall & Co.
P.O. Box 159
Thorndike, Maine 04986
USA
Tel. (800) 223-2336

All our Large Print titles are designed for easy reading, and all our books are made to last.